The
Sensual
Thread

The

Sensual
Thread

a novel by

Beatrice Stone

Third Side Press
Chicago

Cover art copyright © 1994 by Riva Leher
Cover design by Riva Lehrer and Midge Stocker
Interior design and production by Midge Stocker

Printed on recycled, acid-free paper with soy-based inks in the United States of America.

Excerpt from "My Back Door" © 1989 by Melissa Etheridge. Quoted by permission of Rondor Music International.

Library of Congress Cataloging-in-Publication Data
Stone, Beatrice, 1952-
   The sensual thread : a novel / Beatrice Stone. —1st ed.
     p.   cm.
   ISBN 1-879427-18-4
   1. Mountain life—Tennessee—Fiction. 2. Lesbians—Tennessee—Fiction. 3. Time travel—Fiction. I. Title.
PS3569.T6296S76 1994
813'.54—dc20   94-9299
                                      CIP

Third Side Press
2250 W. Farragut
Chicago, IL 60625-1802

First edition, May 1994

10 9 8 7 6 5 4 3 2 1

This book is dedicated to

Dona and Jer,
with thanks for my time on the Mountain,

Melissa, Roey, Anne, and Carol,
with thanks for their support,

And, of course, to Kim,
who made it possible.

Chapter One

Lee slowed the pickup down and felt its automatic transmission shift. The combination of a steep grade and an S-curve forced her to be more careful. A bag of groceries slid across the seat beside her, and a can of fruit rolled into her leg. She grabbed the bag with one hand and righted it, fervently hoping nobody was coming the other way on Rafter Road. Glancing to the left momentarily, she saw the side of the mountain banking precipitously away from the road. On the right was a perpendicular wall of sheer rock.

Lee turned her attention back to driving as the road turned sharply again. A Melissa Etheridge tape played on the cassette player. As a new song began, Lee smiled and joined in softly. This verse had always brought to mind her childhood on the mountain.

> When I was a child I dreamed like a child of wonder, My back in the grass, my eyes to the sky to see, I believed in the stars and I knew that they'd cast the spell that I was under, With my fingers in the dirt I was part of the earth, Every living thing was part of me...

For a second, Lee thought she heard the shrill whistle of a hawk, and her eyes automatically searched the sky. The music throbbed on, drowning out thought and sound. "It's gone gone gone . . ."

Frowning at the repetitive phrase, Lee drove up another hill. Suddenly the truck broke into the open. At the third small plateau, a big clearing really, a couple of houses clung to the side of the mountain. Meadows had been fenced and plowed, and small barns and sheds held a variety of livestock.

She crossed an ancient bridge above the tumbling creek that transversed the meadows. The creek had worn down the mountain, cutting ledges and gaps, depositing dirt and gravel, so that the road was possible. The steep ridges on both sides of the road testified to the feat of engineering the water had performed centuries before settlers had struggled up the mountainside.

Lee turned the truck again as the road twisted upward and out of the meadows. Now a green tunnel surrounded her, rolling and turning constantly upward. Though only in the first week of May, the Tennessee forest displayed the deep, leafy green of summer, with trees and bushes so thick Lee could rarely see back down the mountainside. The traveler couldn't tell how far up the mountain she was until she reached the next plateau.

The truck broke out of the tree-covered road into another clearing. Lee slowed down, surprised to see new rail fences, a new barn, and a remodeled house. This had been just another old homestead five years ago, the last time she had driven this road. Now a small herd of Herefords grazed in one pasture and about half a dozen horses in another.

She pulled over and stopped to take a good look at the horses. Two foals were racing each other around the pasture, while their mothers grazed. A two-year-old filly watched the youngsters, then snorted and cantered after them. Two older geldings joined the game, and soon the whole herd was galloping around the pasture, snorting, tails in the air.

Lee watched with a practiced eye as the horses raced about. They were all quarter horses, obviously well bred and well cared for, Lee thought. They were big and heavily muscled, with some Thoroughbred in their breeding to add height and refinement.

She enjoyed watching all seven horses stretch and play. Nothing could match the thrill she felt watching these born athletes run. The older horses gradually slowed to a trot, then stopped to look around. Seeing nothing to spook at, they began to graze again. Only the two babies continued to play, running, bucking, and kicking as they celebrated the evening.

Lee smiled to herself as she drove on up the road. She might as well admit it. Horses were always going to be important to her, even if she no longer owned one. Lee was thinking about Justin, the beautiful Thoroughbred gelding she had just recently sold, when she realized her turn off of Rafter Road was coming up.

Turning right onto an unmarked dirt road, she drove through a grove of pines. She crossed a small stream and found herself in the sunlight again, and she could see the old wooden fence that marked the edge of her grandmother's property. Before her stretched a narrow valley a half-mile long surrounded by the steep ridges that continued up the mountain. The speeding stream skipped down through the lush meadow that covered the valley floor.

Lee drove down the dirt road toward the farm. She turned into the drive that was overgrown with grass, crossed the stream again, and drove up to the house. Lee stepped out of the pickup and stretched, filling her lungs with pristine mountain air.

She looked around appraisingly. Everything seemed kept up. Aunt Grace had hired a local man to keep tabs on the place and mow around the buildings. It felt almost like Grandma Brant might walk out to say hello any minute.

Lee grabbed her backpack, a bag of groceries, and cane out of the truck. She made sure the house key was in her pocket and then started up the grassy slope to the house. All around her the forest and meadow were celebrating summer's beginning with a bright array of flowers. On the edge of the woods, wildflowers colored the landscape. The honeysuckle bloomed behind the house; its sweet scent filled the evening breeze. The first orange day lily blossoms by the creek were closing. On the gnarled rose bushes beside the porch steps, the first few buds remained open in the golden evening light.

As she reached the porch steps, Lee heard the first whippoorwill call. She stopped to listen. The bird was up in the woods where the shadow of the mountain made night come early. Its call brought back happy memories of summers Lee had spent here on the farm.

She walked up the worn wooden porch steps to the door. Fishing the key out of her pocket, she opened the door and walked into the small house. It smelled musty inside, so Lee left the inside wooden door open. The sweet night air drifted in through the screen door.

Lee walked slowly through the house. Everything was as she remembered it, down to the tiny figurines on the kitchen window. As Aunt Grace had promised, the electricity was on and the phone worked, so she could contact civilization if she ever got the urge.

Finally Lee retraced her steps to the front porch. An old, sturdy rocker there looked inviting, so Lee sat down. Her left leg ached from its injuries, and the other leg complained about the extra load. Was it just her imagination, or did she really feel the pins in her left ankle?

Lee straightened her leg out and tried to get comfortable. She looked out across the sloping front lawn, toward the stream and the road. The only sounds were the wind in the trees and a cowbell clanging somewhere on down the mountain. A dog barked and another, farther away, answered.

"Well, here I am," Lee thought. "Back in the Smokies trying to find the safety and happiness I've always found here. But am I going to be happy here, all by myself?" Lee wondered.

At least she was out of the city and away from the hurry, the stress, and her memories. Lee nodded to herself. She had come a long way today as she had driven south from Cleveland. The Tennessee mountains were a lengthy trip from Ohio, and not just in miles. Lee was aware that she had traveled back in time today too. Maybe here on Grandma's farm she could reconnect with that happier, braver Leah she remembered.

Lee sighed, aware the night was really closing in on the valley. She got up, carefully holding her cane and swung down the steps. Her progress to the truck was slow and painful. Lee gathered the rest of her baggage and started back to the house.

As she reached the porch, Lee heard another whippoorwill call loudly just behind the house. Feeling tired throughout her body, Lee smiled ruefully. At least tonight she would sleep, and even boisterous bird calls wouldn't keep her awake.

♌ ♌ ♌

The next morning Lee slept in late. For the first night in weeks, her sleep had been free of nightmares. Even after the extra sleep, though, twelve hours in the truck the day before left her tired and sore. She struggled out of bed. As she ate breakfast, Lee decided she would take the day off and relax.

Lee checked her groceries. She could make it until tomorrow without buying more supplies. It was a good thing, thought Lee, because she couldn't bear the thought of getting back in that truck today. After rinsing her dishes, Lee wandered onto the front porch. She sat in the rocker and relaxed while she sipped her second mug of tea.

It was a beautiful morning. The sun was bright, and a steady breeze made the air feel fresh and light. Lee noticed marestails in the sky and made a mental note to listen to the weather reports today. Those clouds promised rain and wind tomorrow.

Lee decided to take a walking tour of the property. She changed into her hiking boots and headed out the back door, cane in hand.

Lee's first stop was her Grandma's Concord grape arbor in the backyard. The brown, gnarled vines were beginning to spread their wide, bright green leaves over the wires that formed the arbor. Lee smiled to herself, remembering hiding under the arbor as a child. In the late summer, its green leaves had formed a jade cave where she could hide and eat her fill of the sweet, purple grapes.

She continued up the hill to the edge of the woods. The thick woods formed the back line of the farm clearing and continued up the rugged ridge behind the house. Here, at the edge of the yard, an artesian spring bubbled up out of the ground. The sweet, clear water filled the tank that supplied the house with drinking water, and the overflow formed a brook that tumbled down to join the stream by the road. Beside the spring, a huge old maple stood guard.

The water springing out of the ground had always seemed like magic to Lee. Its twisting journey down the hill had filled her with wonder after Grandma Brant had told her that it was traveling to the sea. Even now, the spring's chuckle made Lee feel like laughing.

She followed the brook down the side of the yard, noticing that watercress was growing along its banks. Here and there tiny wildflowers dotted the grass. The smell of honeysuckle was almost overwhelming as she walked close to the bushes that marked the edge of the yard.

Lee hiked down to the stream by the road. It was hard to walk on the uneven ground, and her cane seemed terribly clumsy. This is just what the doctor ordered, Lee reminded herself. Time to start strengthening her legs, despite the pain and awkwardness, and then she would throw her cane away.

Following the stream across the front of the property, Lee crossed the driveway to the farm. She stopped and looked at the wooden bridge grayed by weathering, that spanned the stream. She remembered her father helping Grandpa Brant secure the heavy locust logs and nail the rough cut lumber on top. Lee continued to stare at the bridge as she thought about her father. She had seen him for the first time in ten years at her mother's memorial service. He had seemed so different, so distant, not knowing how to talk to her or her brother Kenny anymore. L.A. was a long way from Cleveland, Lee told herself. It's a whole different world. It was hard to imagine her father anywhere near this farm now.

Lee walked on toward the barn and sheds. She looked into the chicken coop, surprised to find boxes of canning jars amid the nesting boxes and waterers. The other shed was full of boards and sheets of plywood. Enough wood for all sorts of projects, Lee noted with satisfaction.

Lee went into the lean-to attached to the main barn. There was Amy, Grandpa's old International tractor. It looked like most of his tools were there too, and the bushhog to trim the yard and pastures.

When she walked into the main barn, Lee took a deep breath. A faint smell of corn and hay mixed with the scent of animals. Lee looked around with the eyes of memory, seeing Blackjack, the first horse she ever rode, Grandma's two jersey cows, and the colorful chickens that were always scratching through the dirt on the barn floor. Lee sighed and banished her childhood memories to focus on the present.

Now the barn seemed empty and quiet, the smells just a musty reminder of years past. Lee caught a movement out of the corner of her eye and turned to see a gray tiger cat sneaking away.

"Kitty, kitty," Lee called softly.

The cat paused, looked directly into her eyes, and then slipped into the corn crib. Lee smiled, and walked back outside. At least the buildings were all in good repair, she thought, glad that the barn wasn't just deteriorating the way so many old homesteads did. Even the fences looked in good shape.

Lee continued her walk along the pasture fence, as it slanted uphill to the woods. The pasture continued on for three or four acres to the stand of pines along Rafter Road. The grass was the bright, rich green of early summer, and already over a foot high. Too bad there's nobody to eat it, Lee thought.

She reached the edge of the woods and paused, thinking of the beautiful meadow high on the ridge, but decided it was too much of a climb. She promised herself to visit that favorite spot within the next few days. Then she started back towards the house. Walking on the incline was hard, but the green, living smell of the woods and the scores of wildflowers made it worth the effort. Lee vowed once more to herself to hike up the ridge when her legs were stronger, to visit the secret places of her childhood.

Back at the house, Lee was glad to sit down for a while. Her left leg ached, and even her right leg felt strained. She made herself another pot of tea and relaxed. All too soon the quiet of the house forced her to look for something to do.

For the rest of the day, Lee made herself at home. She unloaded her truck, set up her stereo and typewriter, and hung her clothes. She stacked the books from two big boxes in various places depending on their topics and placed several magazines beside her bed. Some perfunctory dusting was necessary, though the house had stayed amazingly clean.

About five, Lee took time to eat and call Aunt Grace in Knoxville. It was good to talk to someone, and Lee had always loved Aunt Grace. She was surprised to hear herself drawl a bit in response to her aunt's accent. Lee had thought she'd lost all of her childhood Tennessee drawl, but it seemed to crop up at unexpected times.

Lee decided to go to bed early, curling up with the latest copy of *Common Lives*. The quiet of the mountain lulled her to sleep before eleven. She slept through the night undisturbed by dreams.

♌ ♌ ♌

The next morning Lee awoke to a steady drizzle and gray clouds. By noon, when she started the drive down the mountain to town, the wind had picked up, and it was raining hard at times.

It took Lee more than half an hour to drive the ten miles down the mountain and into town. The heavy rain blurred her peripheral vision. Half a dozen times, Lee caught herself looking through the underbrush to see the mountain side fall away below the road. She felt her hands tighten on the wheel and the adrenaline hit her system. She was relieved when she found herself back on flat land.

I've really lost the knack of mountain driving, Lee admitted to herself ruefully. Oh well, practice, practice, she thought, remembering that the drive back up to the farm awaited her.

After shopping for groceries and stopping at the local hardware store, Lee decided she had to find some lunch. She crossed the square and headed for Henry's Restaurant and Sweet Shoppe. As she neared the restaurant, Lee was surprised to find herself afraid to

go inside and sit among so many strangers. She shook
her head and told herself she was being silly.

Lee was about to open the door into Henry's when a
woman stepped out. Lee stood aside and then looked
to see if she recognized the woman. Her inquiring gaze
was met by the bluest eyes she had ever seen. Lee
blinked and smiled in response to the friendly look
and nodded at the young woman as she passed. Lee's
mind whispered a familiar name, but she was uncertain that her memory was correct. It had been so many
years. Lee went in to find a seat, still wondering who
the woman was, and whether she really was an old
friend.

She sat at a small table and Henry came to wait on
her. "Hello Henry."

"Hello miss. Do I know . . . oh it's little Lee Kirby!
Why, I didn't know you were back down here."

"I just got here Monday night. It feels good to be
back at Grandma's."

"Lee, we were all so sorry to hear about your
mother. It must have been hard for you and your
brother, so sudden and all. You were in the accident
too, Grace said."

"Yes, I was driving." Lee's voice was very controlled.

"Oh my. Well . . . say, Kathy, look who's here. It's Lee
Kirby, Ellie Brant's granddaughter."

Kathy, Henry's daughter-in-law, came over to say
hello. She talked a while about several friends Lee remembered fondly, before waiting on other customers.
Eventually Lee ordered the lunch special and got a
chance to eat.

As she paid her bill, Henry started to talk with her
again. "Is your grandma doing all right Lee?"

"Yes. She's in a nursing home near Aunt Grace's
place. I stopped and visited her when I came through
town on Monday. I imagine she'll be up this summer
for a visit."

"Are you staying the summer, then?"

"Yeah, maybe longer. I've decided to write some free-lance articles for a while, while I finish recuperating. Maybe even a book."

"We saw that article you wrote for the Knoxville paper about your grandpa. It was awful funny."

"Well, Grandpa is easy to write about. All I have to do is write down one of his stories."

"He sure was a storyteller. Say, there's another one of you young'uns back on the mountain. Do you remember the Holt girl, Kay Holt? She was leaving just as you walked in the door. She's up off of Rafter Road at her grandma's place. You know, Dixie Holt's place, there on Cemetery Road? You two used to come down here for candy together when you were little."

"That was Kay Holt? I thought I ought to know her. I haven't seen her since we were fourteen."

"She's been here about four years now. She was working with her grandma, learning about healing. Dixie passed last fall, and Kay stayed, trying to carry on. I hear she's got the touch, especially with animals."

"I'll have to visit her sometime."

"Yeah, you girls should reminisce about the old days. Here's your change."

Lee walked out of the bustling Sweet Shoppe and got in her truck. She felt relieved to be out of the restaurant but glad she had talked to Henry. As she headed back up the mountain, she wondered about Kay Holt. They had been so close, sharing all their dreams and secrets. Could they be friends again, Lee wondered, or would their lives be too different after twenty years? Thinking of those friendly blue eyes, she decided to visit Kay soon and at least take a chance at renewing their friendship.

Chapter 2

That evening when the rain slowed to a drizzle, Lee walked out to the barn. She decided to leave her cumbersome cane on the porch.

"Kitty, kitty, kitty," Lee called, then listened for any response. Hearing only the rain, she put down the big ceramic dish of dry cat food she had brought out. At least the skinny tiger could find it there, she thought.

Just as she got back on the porch, Lee heard the telephone ring. She slipped off her soaked shoes and hurried to the phone.

Lee was surprised to hear her friend Sally's voice on the line when she answered.

"Hi Sally."

"I thought I'd surprise you, Lee. How's life on the mountain? Miss Cleveland yet?"

"No, not yet, but it does get pretty quiet here at times."

"So maybe I should come down and escort you to the nearest bar. I suppose that's nowhere near your mountain."

Lee laughed. "No, that'd be in Knoxville, about an hour away. I couldn't guarantee all the glitter of Cleveland."

"Not many towns can," answered Sally with a snort of derision. "So Lee, tell me how you're doing—really. Is it okay there alone? Will you be all right?"

"Yeah Sally, I'm okay. It still feels like it was a good idea to come down. I'd forgotten how beautiful it is here and how much I love it. But tell me what have you been up to? How was your weekend with Debbie?"

Lee and Sally chatted on for several more minutes. After they hung up, Lee felt a little lonely, but it passed. Sometimes it's good to be alone, Lee thought, and then she listened to the night. A nighthawk whistled from close by; then a whippoorwill call pierced the silence. She realized that on the mountain she wasn't alone because so many living beings shared the night with her.

Lee walked out on the porch to retrieve her shoes. It was still sprinkling gently, but the air seemed warmer to Lee. She sat down in the rocker and listened to the rain hit the tin roof of the porch. The wet air seemed saturated with the scents of the plants around the house. If I could bottle this smell, Lee thought, everyone in Cleveland would buy some.

She sat for a while, rocking gently and enjoying the evening. When the mosquitoes began to zero in on her, Lee decided to go back inside. When she stood, she heard a clatter in the barn.

Lee stopped, wondering what to do. That was too much noise for just one cat to make. It's probably a 'coon or 'possum looking around the old grain barrels, Lee speculated. No reason to be afraid.

She had just decided to go to the barn and check out the noise when she heard loud sing-song yowls, the off-key duet of two tom cats insulting each other before their next skirmish. Lee almost laughed aloud at the familiar sounds, glad she didn't have to face a wild animal in the barn. She walked back into the house and sat in the living room. She looked at the bookcase

trying to find a book to read among the titles Grandma
Brant had left there. Maybe Agatha Christie?

Lee paused, thinking about her reactions to the unknown intruder in the barn. Why did the noise scare
her so? It shouldn't. It wouldn't have before. Why was
she always afraid now, waiting for doom to overtake
her? She was acting like a frightened child.

Lee sat back, feeling the familiar blackness come
over her. Depression, self-doubt, criticism, self-analysis,
fear, anger, and guilt all came creeping into her mind,
crowding her thoughts. The pattern was so familiar;
the anxiety and depression were well-known opponents.

Lee shook her head as if trying to clear her thoughts
physically. When that didn't work, she spoke aloud.
"No, I will not let this happen here. I will not be afraid
here. I am safe. I am a whole person here."

In the quiet of the isolated house, her voice reverberated, mocking her. Her heart pounded loudly. Lee shut
her eyes tight, drew a deep breath, and let it out
slowly, trying to center herself.

In the front hall, Grandma Brant's old clock ticked
away the minutes. Outside the whippoorwills called.
The wind stirred the trees on the ridge, and from the
stand of pines came a low, whispering moan. Lee felt
her body relax as her mind quieted. The adrenaline
seeped out of her body, and she felt herself grow tired,
played-out.

Lee picked up the Agatha Christie novel and began
to read. At first the words seemed unrelated and Lee
had to reread several paragraphs. Finally her mind
started to function normally again, and Lee let Agatha
take her elsewhere.

♌   ♌   ♌

That night Lee awoke at three, her heart pounding,
her hands reaching out to ward off an attack. It took

an eternity for her to remember where she was and
identify the shadows around her.

Lee lay in bed wide awake, her breath shallow, her
pulse pounding too rapidly in her ears. She knew all
too well that she must force herself to act normally
and regain control. Bogey men waited for her behind
the doorways of her mind.

Eventually, Lee got up and went to the kitchen. She
turned on the lights and got out milk and cereal.
Nothing was more mundane than eating corn flakes,
Lee reasoned, and it had often helped in the past.

She sat in the kitchen eating, and drinking lots of
milk. Her body relaxed and she began to feel sleepy.
Lee smiled to herself. It was hard to be afraid here,
where she had always felt safe and loved. Soon she
went back to bed and slept again.

During the next week, Lee's life fell into a quiet
routine. She walked every morning, a bit farther every
day. Before lunch she read or did research for her
magazine articles. After lunch she tried to write for
several hours. Then Lee worked outside, planting a
small vegetable garden.

Lee went to town as little as possible. She tried to
envision her life as separate, independent from those
around her. During the day, Lee kept her vision intact,
but at night it was marred by her inner torment.

In the night, Lee couldn't control the access to her
mind. She fought a legion of nightmares and fear that
seemed to march into her thoughts from points unknown. When the terrors of the night started to invade
her daylight hours, Lee decided a change must be made.

I've put myself in a box, Lee admitted to herself. I've
kept my first week here more controlled and limited
than I ever was in Cleveland. I have to start doing what
I want to do, start taking some risks, or I might as
well be back in Ohio holed up in my apartment. Lee
resolved to begin making changes immediately.

She abandoned her routine and drove to Pine Lake
Park that afternoon. She relaxed for some time on the
beach of the park's man-made lake. Later she followed
the hiking trail around the lake, pausing to take photos
often.

The next day Lee decided to go to town and find the
local library. She found it upstairs over the social
security office. The library filled one big room. The
librarian explained that there was a monthly rotation
of books so that new titles were always coming in from
the state library system. Lee got a library card and
checked out several books.

On her way back up the mountain, Lee slowed the
pickup when she reached the farm with the quarter
horses. She had seen a Horse For Sale sign on her way
down, and she was wondering which one was to be
sold. Lee drove into the farm lane, telling herself she
was just going to ask, not buy.

A man in his mid-fifties who introduced himself as
Ralph Hartman answered the door. He came outside to
show her the horses.

"Actually we have two we want to sell," he explained.
"There's a two-year-old filly that's just green broke.
She's got good conformation and is going to make
somebody a great show horse. That's her there."

Mr. Hartman pointed out the sleek bay filly Lee had
seen running in the pasture.

"She sure is a beauty," Lee said with unconcealed
admiration. She watched the filly graze, noticing her
straight legs and balanced muscling.

"She's only green broke? Do you have a horse that's
better trained?" Lee asked.

"Yes, as a matter of fact that's the other one that's
for sale. It's that liver chestnut gelding there. He's
twelve and sound as a dollar. He was my daughter's
horse. She showed him in pleasure and trail classes.
She just got married and moved to Knoxville, so she
wants to sell him. I told her to keep him for her kids,

but she doesn't have any yet. So . . ." Mr. Hartman paused and shrugged.

"Well I imagine she'd enjoy being a bride for a while," Lee observed. "How much is she asking for him?"

"Fifteen hundred. Would you like to see him?" Mr. Hartman asked.

"Sure, why not?" Lee said, telling herself she was just curious.

Mr. Hartman walked into the pasture toward the horses. They all paused to look at him, and both geldings walked toward him. He talked to both of them, scratching the sorrel's neck, and then brought the other gelding to the gate. Lee opened it and let the man and the horse through.

"He's real gentle and almost always comes to you like that. He rides as smooth as any quarter horse I've been on. Do anything you ask, too." Hartman praised the gelding as he held him for inspection.

Lee looked at the gelding, scratched his neck under his mane and talked to him quietly. She walked around him, looking at his legs and feet and tried to get a sense of him.

"Would you like to try him?" Mr. Hartman asked, when she was in front of the horse again.

"Well, I don't know," Lee answered, flustered. "I haven't ridden since I had my accident." She gestured toward her leg.

"Oh—we'll get you up there. After that Ol' Tell will take care of you." Mr. Hartman grinned and started leading the gelding to the barn.

Lee followed, suddenly feeling quite nervous. Yet the chance of being on a horse again after almost a year made her follow Ralph Hartman to the barn.

She helped him brush the gelding and saddle him up. Hartman put an old Western saddle on the horse and a split-ear bridle.

"Here," said Mr. Hartman, "You can use this box to
get up on him."

"I think I'll have to get up on the off side," Lee said.
Mr. Hartman nodded and brought the gelding around
so she could mount him on the right side. Lee felt awkward putting her right leg in the stirrup and swinging
her left leg over the saddle. Although she was mounting on the opposite side than usual, the gelding didn't
bat an eye. He's feeling better about this than I am, Lee
admitted.

In the saddle, Lee shifted around trying to get comfortable. She hadn't ridden Western often, so the big
saddle and long heavy stirrups felt strange. Her left leg
felt stiff and awkward. Her injuries from the car accident had scarred the leg badly, cutting through muscles and nerves, leaving her leg hard to control.

"He neck reins real well. You can take him over there
to the front paddock to ride him." Mr. Hartman
pointed to a big fenced-in area in front of the barn.

Lee walked the horse to the paddock, trying hard to
balance herself in the unfamiliar saddle. So different
from dressage, Lee thought, momentarily remembering
Justin. Of course she wasn't likely to fall off with all
this saddle around her, even if she couldn't squeeze
with her left knee.

Once in the paddock, the gelding moved easily and
Lee knew he was waiting for a cue. She tapped him
lightly with her heal and he broke into a gentle jog
trot. Luckily, a Western jog was slow and even com-
pared to the trot an English horse was asked for, and
Lee sat it easily. Gaining confidence, she trotted around
the paddock in both directions, then asked for a canter.

The gelding answered her cue with a slow lope. He
held his head down, and his lope was a rocking three-
beat gait. Lee rode easily as long as her legs stayed under her, but her left leg gradually moved forward. She
felt her body beginning to bounce forward out of the

saddle, so Lee asked for a walk. The gelding responded
so quickly Lee hit the front of the saddle.

Lee rode for some time, enjoying the feel of a horse
again. She asked the gelding for several maneuvers
and he always complied easily. He's a real athlete, Lee
thought, and he can do more than I can right now.
Finally she rode back to the gate, realizing Mr.
Hartman might be getting impatient.

Ralph Hartman beamed at her, genuinely pleased
that she had enjoyed the ride. He followed her to the
barn and held the horse while she dismounted.

"Nobody'd ever know it's been a while since you
rode," he said with a smile. "You two look good together. He really worked for you."

"Yes, he did." Lee smiled too. She patted the horse
on his neck and told him he'd done well. He turned
and looked at her; his eyes were gentle and knowing.
Lee scratched his neck in response.

"What's his name?" she asked, while she stalled for
time to think.

"His registered name is Tellico Leo Bars. Leo and
Sugar Bars breeding. We just call him Tell, or Tellico."

"You named him for the town?" Lee asked.

"Not exactly," Mr. Hartman explained with a smile.
"*Tellico* means 'chestnut' in Cherokee. That's where
Tellico Plains got its name. We thought with his liver
chestnut color it was real appropriate."

Lee nodded both in response to the story and to herself. She took a deep breath and made an offer.

"I'll give you twelve-fifty for him."

Mr. Hartman nodded. "Done." He smiled at Lee.
"Jenny will be real glad somebody who knows horses
bought him. Do you want us to deliver him to your
place or can you haul him yourself?"

"Well, I thought I'd ride him home in three or four
days. I have to fix up the barn and check the fences. I
live up the road at my Grandma Brant's place," Lee
explained.

"That's fine. Why don't you give me a call when you're ready? Any time is fine. If you want to see him or ride before then, just stop by. We're usually around."

They continued to talk as Lee wrote a check for a deposit. Ralph Hartman was interested in why she had moved to the mountain. He told her about selling his large cattle farm outside Knoxville and moving away from the crowds. Lee told a very abbreviated version of her own story. Finally she left, after talking to Tellico one more time.

I can't believe I did that, Lee said to herself. But I love him; he's so easy to ride. Riding and horses are what I love most, even more than writing. So why not? It's not a question of money or space. Up here is the best place in the world to trail ride. So why not?

Lee laughed aloud. No one was arguing against this! So admit it. You bought a horse because he's wonderful and you love horses. So enjoy.

She drove up to the farm, smiling all the way. It was going to be a great summer.

Chapter 3

Lee spent two days fixing up the barn for her horse.
Cleaning up the stall, repairing it, and buying bedding
kept her busy. She replaced several boards in the stall
and put up a feed tub and big water bucket. After
checking the pasture and fences, Lee was sure there
were no holes or wire lying where Tellico could step
into it. Finally she went to the feed store to stock up
on sweet feed, salt, and other necessities.

At the feed store, she got into a friendly conversation with George Hankey, the young salesman. As they
continued to talk, Lee was amused that he was half-
flirting with her.

"So you're living up on Rafter Road all alone?" he
asked.

"Not exactly. I do have a horse now," Lee answered.

"No husband or boyfriend?"

"No."

"Maybe I should drive up and visit."

"I'm pretty hard to find and it's real quiet up there. I
think you'd find it real boring."

"I would, huh? Maybe you're right. Here's your feed."

He lifted it up into the truck bed. "You might want
to look up that Holt girl. She's got a real nice mare and

all sorts of other animals." He nodded at Lee and
smiled warmly.

As Lee drove up the mountain, she thought about
Kay Holt. Did Kay remember their childhood adven-
tures and adolescent secrets? How had she changed?
She'd have to visit Kay soon, maybe on horseback.

The next day Lee called Ralph Hartman. He agreed to
drive to the farm and pick her up. About fifteen minutes later he arrived and put her new tack in his truck
bed. Lee handed him the final payment on the gelding
as she got into the truck.

As they drove back to his farm, Lee talked about her
visit to the tack shop in the county seat. She'd been
lucky enough to find a well-made, used Western saddle. She'd bought the rest of her tack there, as well as
a couple pairs of heavy-weight jeans for riding. When
they got to his farm, Mr. Hartman helped her tack up
Tellico, adjust the bridle and saddle, and then mount.

"You be careful now, especially up where the road
narrows. Tell is used to cars, so don't worry about him
spookin'. Give me a call when you get there, so I know
you both made it."

"Okay, Mr. Hartman, I'll do that," Lee agreed.

"It's Roger, seeing as we're neighbors. You come visit
us now. My wife wants to meet you too."

Roger Hartman followed her out to the road to see
her off, watching as she urged the horse onto the road.
Lee waved as she headed up Rafter. It would be a long
trip for her because her legs weren't used to riding anymore. Tellico, on the other hand, seemed to be pleased
at the prospect of a ride away from the farm.

The trip was uneventful. They encountered only two
cars, neither at a narrow spot in the road. Lee enjoyed
the slow pace, really observing the rugged beauty
around her.

As Tellico walked along, Lee looked over the edge of
the road down into the steep-sided green valley. She
could see trees clinging precariously to the mountain-

side and surrounded by varied undergrowth. Yellow, pink, and white wildflowers added brilliant dots of color among the multitude of greens and browns. Looking at the myriad of growth Lee was struck by the endless abundance of life all about her. She listened to the constant commentary of hundreds of birds and the buzzing undertone of thousands of insects. Lee smiled wryly and promised herself that she'd never consider the mountains a desolate isolated retreat.

Gazing once more into the forest, she noticed in places the growth was too dense to see far. In other places, she could see down the slope so far that it made her dizzy. She returned her gaze to look at the delicate ferns and the laurel bushes.

We travel too fast, Lee thought. We never get to see most of the natural world. Lee urged her horse off Rafter Road onto the dirt road that led to the farm. Tellico seemed tired, but when they rode out of the pine grove he pricked his ears and started to trot. He seemed to know he was close to home.

At the barn, Lee tied Tellico up and groomed him. She put him in his new stall so he could get used to it. Later she opened the outside door so he could run in and out at will.

As Lee watched, the horse investigated the pasture, whinnying several times, as if he expected to hear nearby neighbors answer him. He walked the fence line for some distance and then wandered over to the middle and started grazing. Lee watched until she was satisfied that Tellico had settled in. Then she went up to the house.

𝒮 𝒮 𝒮

For the next few days, Lee spent a lot of time with her horse. She rode in the pasture and up and down the dirt road. Lee was surprised that the simplest job around the barn was fun.

The chores of feeding and mucking out the stall were added to her daily routine. At first, the hard work made her muscles ache, and gradually Lee found herself enjoying the physical workout. She found that riding and working with Tellico made her days more positive. Writing became fun again, and she felt the quality of her writing improve as well. Lee felt alive again, enjoying her visit to the mountains instead of existing in an isolated camp.

After several days, Lee decided to ride over to find Kay Holt. She talked to Tellico about Kay as she saddled up, explaining that Kay and she were old friends. Lee wondered aloud whether Kay knew she was on the mountain, or even remembered her at all.

"Surely she must," Lee said to Tellico, trying to reassure herself. No one would forget all those good times, even after twenty years. Tellico's ears twitched back and forth as he listened to Lee's monologue. Lee wondered what he thought of her uneasiness.

They went down Rafter Road to a dirt road that climbed steeply up a ridge. A sign pointing the way to Pine Ridge Cemetery provided the direction Lee was looking for. She urged Tellico up the steep grade when he hesitated, so he gamely lengthened his strides. Lee heard rocks shifting under his hooves and realized the edge of the road hadn't been packed down much this spring. She decided to let Tellico pick his own speed so he wouldn't stumble.

As they rounded the next turn, the cemetery came into view. It was a small graveyard filled with the headstones of mountaineers dated as early as 1850. No sign of the small wooden chapel that had stood in the clearing for over a century was visible. The huge, old loblolly pines that gave the spot its name were bent and twisted in the same direction as the prevalent winds. The late morning breeze made the big trees whisper, as their long needles moved in the wind. Lee stopped to listen, wishing she could understand what they were saying.

Lee turned Tellico away from the cemetery to the narrow path that led to the Holt farm. There was a Jeep parked at the end of the cemetery road, and Lee assumed it was Kay's. It was obvious no one drove up to the farm anymore.

She urged Tellico on as he paused to sample the leaves of a bush. The path led upward about twenty yards through an old stand of hardwoods interspersed with blooming mountain laurel. Then Lee rode into a large clearing. Directly ahead was the old Holt farmhouse and barns.

Lee stopped Tellico, staring in amazement. Between them and the house was a big stump, and Kay Holt was sitting on it, obviously waiting.

"Hello, Lee," Kay said with a wide smile. "I've been waiting for you all morning, and I thought I'd better be here to welcome you."

"Hi." Lee was taken aback by the statement but warmly accepted Kay's welcome. "I'm glad to see you Kay. But how did you know I was coming?"

Kay laughed easily and jumped down off the stump. "Everyone I know in town has been telling you to visit me. And today felt like the right day. When I heard the crows call in the cemetery, I knew you were practically here. Come on, bring your horse over to the barn and we'll give him a rest while we talk."

Lee nodded and followed Kay to the barn. She started to dismount and almost lost her balance on the uneven ground. She felt Kay's hands grab her waist and steady her. Kay took Tellico's reins without comment while Lee loosened the saddle girth. She gave Lee a rope to tie the gelding with and showed her a stall to put him in.

"Come on up to the house. I have some iced tea made, and we can have some sandwiches for lunch if you like," Kay offered.

"Sounds good," agreed Lee, realizing she was hungry. In the house Lee smiled in recognition and turned to Kay. "It all looks just like I remember it from when we were kids. It's like Grandma Brant's place, all so familiar and safe."

Kay chuckled, "Well I did make a few changes. I brought up my stereo and TV. Of course the television is practically useless and I had to put up an outside antenna to pick up any radio stations. Maybe I should have sold them, but I do enjoy my tapes and albums.

"The rest of the house is pretty much the same. Grandma knew what she needed to live here comfortably, and I agree with most of her choices.

"Come into the kitchen and we can have some tea."

Lee followed Kay into the kitchen and sat down at the old cherry table. Dried herbs hung by their stems all around the ceiling, and jars full of ground leaves and seeds filled the shelves. Lee remembered the kitchen's smell from years before, almost like the woods in autumn, but spicier.

Kay poured two big glasses of iced tea and put sprigs of mint into them. She sat down opposite Lee and raised her glass.

"Here's to old friends," she said.

Lee smiled, raised her glass, and took a sip. Not just tea, but a luscious mixture of tea and fruit juices filled her mouth. Why did everything seem like a wonderful surprise today?

Kay smiled again and seemed pleased to have her there. Lee took the time to look at her childhood friend and found her even more beautiful than she remembered. Beautiful? No, handsome or striking would be a better description.

Kay's hair was black and tied back in long braids. One unruly strand tucked behind her ear was streaked with gray. Her complexion was darkened by the sun with a few freckles on her nose. Her high, prominent cheekbones spoke of her Cherokee heritage, but her

brilliant blue eyes twinkled in Dixie Holt's image. Lee
found it hard to look away from those eyes.

"We have a lot to catch up on," Lee said, trying not
to stare at Kay any longer.

"Yes, it's been twenty years, hasn't it? Funny how I
remember that time we spent together so well." Kay
smiled easily, and Lee felt herself relax.

"I wish we could have kept writing, but I guess that's
just hindsight," Kay continued. "Did you become a history teacher or a writer?"

Lee smiled pleased that Kay had remembered.

"A writer. I was working for *Ohio Heritage* magazine
in Cleveland, so I managed to combine them. What
about you? Did you study medicine or become a
biologist?"

"Both. I studied as an osteopath for almost two
years before I decided that herbal medicines were less
intrusive. I worked with a woman in Oregon for a
while, then came back to study with Grandma. She
had so much of the old knowledge and skill, and I
was very lucky to work with her as long as I did."

"I was told you have the touch, Kay," Lee said. "That
means a lot here. Especially with animals, Henry said."

"Henry always was the town crier. I do a lot of work
with animals and sometimes with people. It takes a
while to gain people's confidence—no matter whose
granddaughter you are." Kay smiled again but not so
easily this time.

"As I rode here I kept wondering if you remembered
those days we ran all over the mountain, and all our
secret places?" Lee paused, suddenly not certain how
to continue.

"Of course I do. That was part of what brought me
back," Kay assured her.

Lee met Kay's eyes once more and felt a thrill. This
is crazy, she said to herself. You're not fourteen anymore, and this woman is not someone to develop a
crush on.

They had both finished their tea, and Kay suggested
they go relax in the living room. Lee sat down at one
end of the couch, and Kay walked over to the stereo to
put on a tape.

"What kind of music do you like?" Kay asked.

Lee was about to say something totally inane and
then decided to tell the truth.

"I listen to women's music. Singers like Ferron and
Lucie Blue Tremblay."

Kay nodded and pushed a button. The opening
chords of "Strange Paradise" filled the room.

"That's Cris Williamson." Lee was startled.

Kay grinned. "I thought you might know the tune.
I've been wondering for years if you came out. You
looked mighty dykey in town, but I wasn't really sure
until today."

"Am I that obvious?" Lee asked with a smile,
although she was surprised.

"Only to another lesbian," Kay laughed warmly.

The conversation paused for a moment and Lee took
the opportunity to gaze about the room. Old, well-worn
furniture in tones of blues and grays sat in long-
accustomed spaces. A hand-carved butter bowl, a
wooden mortar and pestle, a hand-thrown vase, and
a handful of arrowheads were placed about the room.
Two walnut bookshelves Lee remembered from years
past were filled with herbals, the *Foxfire* books, and
various medical and veterinarian references. Beside
her, a beautiful burl oak end table that the years had
graced with a rich patina held an old family bible and
a vase of red roses. The overall effect of the muted
colors and wood was a quiet room where a body could
relax and be at peace.

"So what have you done over the years?" Kay asked.

"Well, I guess I can tell you the unedited story of my
life," Lee said.

"Please."

"I came down for the next two summers after you left. When Mom and Dad started having major problems, I stayed up in Ohio except for a week or two each year. Dad left when I was 17, and I didn't see much of him after that." Lee paused wondering what else to say.

"Where did you go to college?" Kay asked.

"Oberlin. It's a small school near Cleveland."

"Hmm, that sounds familiar. Why would I recognize the name?" Kay frowned, trying to remember.

"Well, it's got a rather radical reputation and a great music department. It was also the first coed school," Lee answered.

"That must be it. Women's Studies 101 trivia. I took a couple courses at UCLA and found the Women's Center." Kay chuckled as she remembered her college days. "I kept going there, hoping to meet other lesbians. Finally I saw a notice for a lesbian support group. It took me over a week to get up the nerve to call."

Lee joined in her comfortable laughter.

"Did you come out at college, Lee?" Kay asked.

"Not at Oberlin. Actually I had a rather passionate affair when I was a senior in high school. I told myself I was just in love with another person who happened to be a woman."

"That sounds familiar," Kay nodded. "When did you decide otherwise?"

"I found the Women's Center, too. And all these wonderful outspoken women were saying things I agreed with. We all went to a Meg Christian concert and I saw the light."

"I can imagine. All those dykes singing 'Leaping Lesbians.'"

"Yeah, and we all had our arms around each other, swaying back and forth." Lee laughed. "It was a mystical experience."

"Very moving, no doubt." Kay grinned, her blue eyes twinkling.

"Very."

"Did you start working right after you graduated?"

"No, I got an assistantship at Indiana University in Bloomington. I was there for two years and got my master's. Then I went back to Cleveland to work on the magazine."

"Did you resign before you came down, or are you writing for the magazine this summer?"

"No, I resigned." Lee hesitated, then decided to explain. "After the accident I took a leave of absence for six months. I went back to work, but somehow it had become really trivial—at least it felt that way. I felt like I'd been getting caught up in my career and losing my perspective. That's why I came down here for a few months, to try and regain some balance. I've got a couple of freelance assignments from my old editor to work on. In fact I have to finish one up tonight."

"What's it about?" Kay asked with obvious interest.

"It's on Conrad Richter and his book *The Trees*. It's about the early settlement of Ohio. I just have to do a final draft tonight and get it in the mail."

For a moment their conversation halted. Lee looked back at Kay, finding a mixture of uncertainty and sorrow on her face.

"What?" she demanded softly.

"I read about your accident in the paper. I was sorry to hear about your mother. I always remember her as so kind and funny. I wanted to say something to offer my sympathy, but I don't know how. It must have been so hard."

"It was." Lee stopped, her thoughts turned inward.

Kay waited quietly until she was sure Lee wanted to continue talking. Her blue eyes seemed gentle and kind when Lee returned from her momentary reverie.

"You must miss Grandma Dixie, too."

"Yes, there's times when I find myself expecting her to answer my questions," Kay confided. "But she had lived a long and very happy life. It wasn't sudden or unexpected. We both were preparing for her death for a long time. In many ways, Grandma's dying helped me understand and value life much more."

Kay smiled slightly as if acknowledging the discussion had become too intimate for Lee's first visit. She changed the subject.

"Do you want some lunch? There's some tuna salad in the refrigerator. If you're a vegetarian, there's some fruit and cheese I can dig out," Kay offered.

"Tuna's fine," Lee agreed. "I always feel guilty about eating meat. At least I don't devour sixteen-ounce sirloins any more."

Kay laughed. "Who can afford them?"

After lunch they went outside to see Kay's mare. As they walked through the barnyard, Lee was struck by the timelessness of the farm. It seemed exactly as she remembered it from twenty years before, and it was beautifully kept up.

Kay's horse was in a small paddock beside the barn. Climbing red roses wove around several sections of the fence up to the gate. When Kay's coal black mare looked over the gate, Lee felt like she was looking at a painting.

"She's beautiful, Kay. What's her breeding?"

"She's a Morgan. I bought her two years ago as a two-year-old. I took one look at her and fell in love. Her name is New Moon Dancer, I call her Dancy. I always wanted a black mare."

"She sure has class. Will you breed her?"

"Probably, if I can find the right stallion. Right now I just love riding her. We'll have to go trail riding sometime. There's those wonderful old logging roads all through the mountains that we explored on Blackjack."

"I'd love it, as long as we start out easy. My legs need to be built up," Lee said cautiously.

"How about tomorrow? I'll pack a lunch," Kay suggested enthusiastically.

"What time?"

"Is seven too early? I have to see a couple of people in the afternoon."

"Sounds great. It's cooler then anyway."

Kay smiled warmly, looking directly at Lee. Lee felt another twist inside as she looked back into those deep blue eyes. This time she just let herself enjoy the feeling.

They talked on for some time about horses, a mutual love. Lee told Kay about her dressage training and her sadness at selling her big gelding. Kay understood and supported her decision to buy Tellico.

"Horses are necessary to some people. I think it's an inborn thing that other people can't understand. It's like explaining to a New Yorker why you live in the mountains," Kay theorized to Lee. "You need that gelding to keep yourself sane. Besides he's a good investment at that price. He's worth at least twice that in Knoxville. Ralph must like you; he's usually real sharp."

Lee smiled her agreement and nodded. She glanced at her watch and couldn't believe it.

"I've got to go Kay. It's almost three. I have a deadline on that damn article, so it has to go in tomorrow's mail." Lee's voice underlined her disappointment.

"Well I'm glad you came up. It's great to talk to an old friend, especially if she's a dyke, too." Kay grinned.

Lee found herself smiling back. She was beginning to look forward to that grin and the twinkle in Kay's eyes that accompanied it.

They went into the barn and brought Tellico out. Kay tightened the girth and checked his bridle. Lee moved to Tellico's right side, then hesitated, uncertain whether she could mount unassisted. Kay moved to the horse's off side next to her. Seeing Lee hesitate about mounting, she extended her hands.

"I'll give you a leg up."

"Okay," Lee said. When she put her bent knee into Kay's cupped hands, Kay threw her up easily.

"Do you always throw women around that easily?" Lee asked quizzically from up in the saddle. "Whenever possible. I always enjoy having a woman in my hands," Kay answered solemnly but her eyes danced merrily. Lee turned to leave reluctantly, but Tellico was glad to go. He ambled unasked into a trot. Lee turned to wave goodbye and the clearing was gone, lost behind the huge, old trees.

Chapter 4

The next morning Lee rode up the path from the cemetery at exactly seven o'clock. She had to admit that she was even more nervous about this second visit with Kay than she had been the day before. The alarmed caws of the crows sounded abrasive echoes of the near panic she felt as she approached the Holt farm.

Why, what's so different from yesterday, Lee asked herself. Seeing Kay's face in her mind's eye, Lee smiled at herself. You're going to see another lesbian, a woman you find terribly attractive and exciting. That's a valid reason for being nervous, so just accept it and enjoy the day. Lee was firm with herself as Tellico walked into the farm clearing.

Lee saw Kay leading her black mare out of the barn and mounting quickly.

"Just stay there Lee. We'll ride down to the cemetery first," Kay called.

Tellico shifted restlessly under Lee as Kay rode Dancy toward them. He was glad to see another horse but unsure of the mare's temperament. Both he and Lee were relieved to see that Dancy didn't pin her ears or make any threatening gesture as they rode side-by-side down to the cemetery.

They rode in silence past the cemetery, then on to
the dirt rode that turned up the ridge. Almost immediately there was a Y in the road. One branch was fairly
well traveled with hard-packed dirt and rocks making
up the roadway. Kay pointed to the other branch that
appeared to continue up the ridge. It was overgrown
with grass and weeds yet easily followed.

"Let's go this way, Lee. The other road just rejoins
Rafter eventually. We can see a great view from up on
the ridge, and there's a wonderful grove where we can
stop and eat, too."

Lee nodded agreement and Kay started up the road
with Tellico following close on Dancy's heels. Lee felt
the gelding move easily under her, the angle of the
slope negated by his well-conditioned body. Lee was
glad to have a big Western saddle to hold her firmly as
they continued upward. Her knees and thighs were nowhere near as ready for the climb as Tellico was.

In a few minutes, Lee relaxed enough to look around
and enjoy the rugged scenery. Here and there a few
huge trees clung to the ridge. The other trees were
smaller, obviously second growth, and surrounded
by laurel bushes and undergrowth. The laurel was
beginning to blossom, its big pink and white flowers
voluptuous against the woodland backdrop. Elsewhere
feather-like ferns and delicate wildflowers spread dis-
creetly across the forest floor. In many areas the
woods seemed dark and shadowy, hiding itself from
prying eyes. Here and there sunlight streamed down
through the green density of the leaves above, making
a yellow speckled pattern on the undergrowth. The yellow spots danced as the morning breeze moved
through the leaves above.

Lee took a deep breath, inhaling the woods as its
mixed odors mingled with the sweaty scent of Tellico
and her body. The smells of the forest always brought
colors to mind, Lee thought: the deep green smell of
the trees; the sharper, lighter green, almost acidic

smell of the underbrush; and the rich, musky browns
of the damp dirt, mushrooms, and decayed leaves.

Lee looked ahead and realized Kay was waiting for
her to catch up. As Lee came up beside her, Kay asked
Dancy to keep pace with Tellico.

"You looked happy, very much a part of the forest,"
Kay began.

Lee nodded. "I like the quiet."

"Yeah. I always feel all of me relaxes in the woods,
as if my body takes on a slower, deeper rhythm. Sometimes it helps to be far away from other people."

Lee nodded again and remained silent. They continued to ride side-by-side, the easy silence between them
just part of the natural quiet of the forest.

But it isn't all that quiet, Lee thought to herself as
she listened. There were the sounds of the horses as
they moved, the creaks of the saddles, and the whisper
of the trees above. Lee listened intently to be more
aware of the forest sounds. She could hear the constant hum of thousands of insects and the more distinct calls of dozens of birds. Here and there a
chipmunk scrambled and a squirrel scolded. Occasionally there was the rustle of a larger animal pushing
through the undergrowth, startled into movement by
the sounds and scents of horses and humans on the
logging road.

They rode into a small area where the road was
wider and the ridge fell away steeply on one side. From
atop their horses, they were high enough to look down
the mountainside, as it fell away seemingly untouched
beneath them.

Lee felt herself sway, a little dizzy, as she looked
into the mist-filled valley. The forest's stillness filled
her soul with an all-encompassing green light. Then
she heard a whistle-cry. Looking outward she saw a red-
tailed hawk circling, riding the thermals upward.

She watched the bird in silence, then looked down
again, this time through the hawk's eyes. The wind

played around her feathered face, promising her access to all the mountainside below her. She focused her golden eyes to look past the treetops, down to the forest floor. The rocks, leaves, and laurel hid her prey, but only momentarily. There was a movement and a flash of gray fur as a mouse ducked under a leaf. She adjusted her flight and her eyes focused sharper as she prepared to hurtle earthward.

Lee jumped when she heard Kay's quietly insistent voice. "Come back, hawk-woman."

Lee turned to see Kay watching her intently. She was surprised to feel Tellico under her.

"You can still fly with her then?" Kay asked. "I didn't know if you would remember how."

"I didn't either," said Lee in an unsettled voice.

She had almost forgotten this secret, once so precious, now almost feared. It was too close to her dreams. She asked Tellico to walk on, not wanting to talk any more about it. Kay respected her silence.

♌ ♌ ♌

They had been riding for an hour and a half when Lee realized they were close to the top of the mountain. They came out into a small meadow that had only an old stone chimney and a huge, old lilac bush as reminders of the homesteader who had cleared the land. Lee turned her gelding so she could see the view that Kay felt was worth such a long ride.

Below her the was the side of the mountain they had just ridden up. Lee looked at the green canopy that fell away steeply. The green treetops were endless. Some varied in shape and color, but nowhere could Lee pick out any evidence of the farms that dotted the mountainside. Lee looked both right and left and saw the endless procession of tree-covered peaks that crossed the landscape on a slight angle across the entire state. And on north to Maine and south to Georgia, Lee

reminded herself, looking at the mountains to the
south swaddled in low clouds.

"Was it worth the ride?" Kay asked quietly.

"Oh, yes," Lee breathed, as her eyes swept once
more along the pristine landscape. For several minutes
both women remained silent, their minds traveling
through the mountain ridges about them.

"There's an inscription on the chimney, if you want
to see," Kay offered.

"Sure."

Kay swung easily off Dancy and stood by Tellico's
offside as Lee dismounted. Lee was glad to have her
steadying hand as she took an unsteady first step, her
muscles protesting the ride.

They walked to the back of the old chimney, leading
the horses by their reins. Kay bent down and pulled
back a bush exposing a flat, slate stone three feet from
the ground. Lee looked closely to comprehend the
blurred inscription as Kay read it aloud.

"God Bless this House, John Moses Holt, Martha
Kirby Holt, May 21, 1838." Kay smiled up at Lee. "We
aren't the first Holt and Kirby to know one another.
These two built here as the Cherokees were moved
west. My father was a direct decendent of John Moses
Holt, and Martha Kirby was a cousin of yours."

Lee touched the cool stone of the chimney, wondering aloud what that couple had looked like and how
they had lived in such an isolated spot. To her mind
came an instantaneous picture of a dark-haired wiry
man heaving against a huge stump, while a blond
woman urged on a team of two brown mules that were
trying to pull the stump from the ground. Sweat
dripped off all four figures, and both the man and the
woman looked exhausted. Lee shook her head, denying
the image.

"Did you see?" asked Kay, looking steadily at Lee.

"No, of course not. . . ." Lee looked into Kay's serene
blue eyes and realized she expected the truth. Lee also

understood that somehow Kay already knew the answer. Lee decided to admit it.

"Yes, you're right. I saw them working to clear the land. How did you know?"

"It was in your face, like someone watching a movie. Besides I've see you do it before, remember? That's something that's hard to forget."

"I'd forgotten—almost."

Kay cocked her head slightly, as if listening to a more involved explanation, then nodded.

"We can eat here or ride to the grove. It's about ten minutes' ride from here."

"Let's ride."

Kay tossed Lee easily into her saddle and then mounted Dancy herself. They rode down through the meadow and onto the logging road.

Lee rode beside Kay, but Kay's focus seemed elsewhere. She seemed unaware of Lee's questioning glance, so Lee took the opportunity to observe Kay as she rode.

Lee looked at her old friend in puzzlement. What could Kay be thinking so hard about? In a moment, Lee found her own mind shifting as she looked at Kay appraisingly. Kay was slightly taller than Lee and much more muscular. Lee watched with pleasure as Kay rode with unthinking grace, an extension of the mare below her. Lee was watching the movement of Kay's strong hands on the reins when she was startled by Kay's voice. Lee glanced upward to find Kay regarding her.

"We turn in here and follow the stream down." Kay's eyes danced at her as Lee felt herself blush.

They rode close to the streambed, dodging tree limbs and bushes. Suddenly the underbrush was gone and a grove of tall pines surrounded them. Lee looked ahead and saw the stream had been blocked by a fallen tree. It formed a pool of dark, cool water at the edge of the pine grove.

"This is beautiful, Kay. I'll never question your decisions again, at least about trail riding."

Kay grinned and swung down off her mare. Lee waited for her to come to Tellico's side in case she needed help, then dismounted too. Kay's hands steadied her again, then held her tightly just a moment too long. Lee smiled to herself as she tied Tellico to a tree with a rope and loosened his saddle.

Kay had spread out the lunch she had packed. Sandwiches, oranges, and some cookies, as well as a Thermos of tea, looked inviting to Lee although it was only nine o'clock. She sat down and began to eat.

"Did you enjoy the ride up? Was it too long?" Kay asked.

"No, it wasn't too long. It was well worth it, although I'll probably pay for it tomorrow. How did you ever find this spot?"

"Grandma showed it to me years ago. I always wanted to show it to you when we were teenagers, but it was too far for old Blackjack, so we didn't have a way to get here."

"Did she show you the chimney too?"

"No, I found that myself. Then I found John Moses Holt in the family bible, but Martha Kirby was harder. I had to check the county history books for her."

"She was mentioned there?" Lee was astonished.

"As a footnote. One of her sons helped build the local railroad."

They sat quietly for several minutes finishing their brunch. Lee enjoyed the silence and knew neither of them found it uncomfortable.

"What's it like to be a lesbian up here in the mountains? Is there a social life at all? Are you out to anyone?" Lee asked, her voice slightly restrained by the mountain quiet.

Kay finished her tea before answering.

"I'm out to a few people, but I think most of my friends assume I'm a hermit. It's not really a problem.

There are a few other lesbians around, mostly couples. We get together sometimes, and I've seen a couple women since I've been here."

"Anyone special?"

"Not yet."

Kay smiled faintly at Lee, then looked away. Quiet settled between them again. After a few minutes, Kay started to pack up the lunch remains.

"We'd better head back. I've got people to see this afternoon and some typing to do tonight," Kay suggested.

"Okay."

Once again they were back on their horses and riding down the logging road. Lee became determined to generate some conversation. She was about to ask more questions when Kay's voice interrupted her thoughts.

"I'm sorry I've been so quiet today. I'm so used to riding in the mountains by myself that talking seems almost sacrilegious. I was going to tell you more about the other women around, if you're interested."

"That'd be great."

"Let's see. I know of three couples fairly close by that I've become friends with. Mary and Fran run a small inn just across the North Carolina line. Susan and Martha live up by Gatlinburg on a farm. Susan's the farmer, and Martha's an artist. She sells pieces in the stores at Gatlinburg and Pidgeon Forge. Then there's Margarette and Toni who live in Madisonville and work at the hospital.

"We get together sometimes to celebrate the holidays. Usually in the winter, since summer is busy for all of us. Last year all eight of us had a huge Thanksgiving dinner at Mary and Fran's. Theirs is the only place with a big enough table. I try to keep in touch all year, but sometimes it's hard."

"Are there many single women nearby?" Lee asked, taking the bull by the horns.

"A few. I met people by leaving a note at the
Women's Center in Knoxville and writing to *Lesbian
Connection*. Like I said, I've seen a couple of women
here, but it never lasted. Terry lives in Madisonville
too. We still see each other occasionally, but she
spends a lot of time in Knoxville now."

Kay fell silent again, and Lee pondered over the elusive Terry and how Kay felt about her. Kay interrupted
her thoughts once more.

"Why do you ask Lee? Are you getting bored with
living on the mountain already?"

Kay's teasing grin reassured Lee as she was about to
challenge the question. She decided on the direct approach instead. "Actually, I was trying to find out if
you were involved with someone now."

Kay's laugh echoed back to them from the ridge
walls. "You're interested?" Kay was still chuckling.

"Yes," Lee answered simply, trying to control her
blush. She glanced sideways just in time to see Kay's
wide grin and notice a suspicious reddening under her
tan.

This exchange seemed to clear the air, and the two
women talked and laughed all the way down the mountain. As they talked, Lee decided Kay had been just as
nervous this morning as she was, and for the same reasons. She was surprised at how soon they reached the
cemetery and disappointed to see Kay turn her black
mare toward the farm.

Then Kay halted Dancy and turned back toward Lee.
"I'll call you tomorrow night. I'll be in Madisonville all
day, but maybe we can get together on Thursday."

"Sounds good," Lee answered.

She watched Kay and the black mare disappear up
the path, then turned to ride home.

ℒ ℒ ℒ

The rest of the day was anticlimactic for Lee. She tried to write but found her thoughts drifting back to her morning ride. She started to read an article that had sounded fascinating when she copied it, but after the third attempt to read the first page she put it down. Kay's grinning face kept appearing as Lee wrote a letter to her Grandmother Brant. She gave up the fight and wrote a detailed account of her two visits with Kay. Grandma will be delighted, Lee assured herself, remembering that Dixie Holt had been Ellie Brant's best friend.

When Lee still found herself speculating on Kay's trip to Madisonville, she became disgusted. She decided to work outside in the garden until dark to keep her mind and body busy.

That night Lee was awakened by her dreams. She was very drowsy and tried to fall back asleep, but her mind rebelled and kept reviewing an experience she had had more than a year before. It happened two months before her mother's death, but it had been one of the reasons she had escaped to the mountains. The sequence in the bar was all too familiar and still filled her with panic.

Lee and her three friends had eaten out at a nice restaurant and then gone on to the bar. For dessert Lee had drunk a White Russian, and at the bar she decided to try another. The night had been fun and the drinks were cheap, so Lee kept reordering. It was after her second refill, when she walked back to the restroom, that she realized how drunk she was.

But it was a different feeling, Lee decided, as she nursed that final drink along. The vodka had hit her hard, but the rich cream had masked some of the unpleasant side effects of intoxication. Lee found herself looking around the bar and at her friends with a detached analytical air that threatened to turn into either depression or sleep from moment to moment.

Lee had looked at the bartender, an older woman
who worked amazingly quickly and always had a smile
or laughing comment ready for everyone.

"I wonder how you really feel tonight, what it feels
like for you to tend bar on a Friday night," Lee had
muttered just under her breath. No one had heard her
through the music and laughter.

Suddenly Lee was behind the bar mixing a scotch
and water. The air was unbearably smoky and hot. Her
feet ached and so did her head. She was tired after
working all day in the typing pool and wished it was
last call instead of just after midnight. The women's
orders seemed unending, but she knew from experience to take them one at a time so she could make it
through the night. She wondered how her lover, Mary,
was doing at home with their daughter, Heather, who
had the measles. Above all she wanted to go home to
bed.

When Lee's mind returned to its normal vantage
point, Lee had been startled yet delighted at this new
trick of her imagination. No doubt the alcohol had
freed her from some inhibitions to let her imagination
take her away like that. Then Lee noticed the bartender
serve what looked like a scotch and water to a waiting
customer, and how she had massaged her temple before turning to mix another drink. For a moment Lee
felt a touch of fear, but she pushed it aside.

Dismissing her trepidation as foolish, Lee had looked
elsewhere to continue her fascinating new game. There
at the bar was Cindy Shepard, a nodding acquaintance from her days at Oberlin. Lee had always been
attracted to Cindy but afraid of her seemingly unassail-
able reserve. Cindy had seen Lee and smiled hello, then
turned back to her drink. Lee decided she'd let her
imagination play with Cindy for a few minutes.

"How does Cindy feel tonight about being here, and
seeing me?" Lee had said in an undertone.

She was Cindy for a few seconds, sipping a drink that was just a Coke and wishing she hadn't come to the bar alone. She had been glad to see Lee there and wished Lee was with mutual friends so she would feel comfortable about going over. She'd love to dance with Lee; she was such a sexy dancer. She'd love to know her better. Cindy couldn't understand why anyone with so much talent and ability would end up drinking and smoking her life away. She wondered briefly what Lee was like in bed, then discarded the notion as ridiculous. She had just decided to leave when a familiar voice said hello.

Lee had returned to her own body and mind, feeling embarrassed and ashamed. It was as if she had overheard a conversation about herself, a very negative conversation. Lee knew her face was bright red, and all she could think of was going home. She leaned over to tell her friends she was leaving. They nodded, unconcerned. As she left, Lee noticed Cindy watching her and then turning back to a mutual friend from college.

The memory ended as Lee got in her car and was very aware that the drive home would be hard in her drunken condition. She remembered feeling like she was going to throw up. Then she became aware of the silence of the mountain night.

Lee sat still, hugging herself, trying to lose her fear and depression in the reality of the present. She forced herself to get up.

In the kitchen Lee drank a big glass of milk and tried to read a short story. After ten minutes or so, her mind was more orderly and her body more relaxed. Then Lee went back through her memories, trying to think through the incident at the bar.

Why had she been focusing on it tonight? Why was she so frightened? Why had her memory included details that made her imaginings seem even more real? She had always assumed it was a weird form of para-

noia that she had experienced that night, as it had
been on other drunk or stoned occasions.

Lee stopped and suddenly saw Kay's open face before her as Kay had asked about the vision beside the
chimney. Kay had accepted it as real, or at least as a
valid experience. She also seemed to accept the strange
happenings that had visited them both in adolescence.
Was this other experience, this reaching into another's
mind, just as valid?

Lee found herself unable to answer that question, so
she posed another. Why had she been so frightened
that night in the Cleveland bar? Why had that memory
frightened her so tonight? It was more than embarrass-
ment at being judged, more than the shame of acknowledging her self-destructive lifestyle. What had it been?

Lee's mind searched through the memory again,
unable to generate an answer. She thought of those
adolescent experiences with Kay that were carefully
buried deep in her memory. She picked up a pen and
doodled on a notepad while she thought.

She and Kay had become incredibly close those last
two summers on the mountain. They spent all their
time together, sharing their imaginations, dreams,
and fears. The last summer they had crossed a line
together. They were more than friends but afraid to
act out their love.

Strange feelings arose; energy crackled between
them that went unspent. They began to answer each
other before the question was asked. They knew when
and where to find each other at any time of the day.
They began to crave the same foods, dream the same
dreams, and laugh together at unspoken jokes. When
Lee had hugged Kay, they both felt the need between
them. At summer's end, when Kay had finally kissed
Lee, Lee had felt the power between them that drew
them together. She had later dismissed it as blooming
sexuality, but now she wasn't so sure.

Lee looked down at her doodle. She had drawn a circle with one firm line and then had begun scribbling over it, blurring the edges. Blurred edges, blurring her own edges? Lee asked herself. Losing track of one's self while loving another was a common enough fear, one that Lee had worked through many times. But why was it here, now?

Lee tried to think but found herself yawning uncontrollably. Maybe this could wait until tomorrow, she decided, and stumbled into bed. Her sleep was deep and undisturbed.

Chapter 5

The next day was easier for Lee. Kay still appeared in her imagination often, but her mind was more controlled. She was able to read and work on an article. In the afternoon, she rode Tellico down the road just to loosen her sore muscles.

At eight the phone rang. Lee knew it wasn't Kay but couldn't imagine who else would call. Her friend Sally's voice was a welcome surprise. They each talked about their week, and Sally shared her delight with a new love affair. She kept talking about Debbie until Lee mentioned Kay; then Sally started a spate of questions and jokes about rekindling a teenage romance. Lee was still laughing when she hung up.

It was ten-thirty when Kay called. Lee answered, aware that her tone was too pleased as she responded to Kay's low voice. She was wondering why everything Kay did seemed incredibly sexy to her, and almost missed the invitation to go swimming the next day.

"I thought we could go down to the river, unless you like the state park beach?" Kay asked, her husky tones thrilling Lee.

"The river sounds great. What time?"

"How about one? We can keep cool through the hottest part of the day that way. Bring some sneakers to wear in the river. The rocks can be sharp."

"I'll be looking forward to it."

Kay answered with a yawn, and they ended their conversation. Lee continued to think about her reaction to Kay as she got ready for bed. Once in bed she was restless, finding her mind settling on Kay again. She began to wonder how it would feel to have Kay touch her or kiss her, when she stopped herself.

This was crazy to be fantasizing about someone she didn't know at all. That wasn't quite true, she admitted, but it was close enough. Lee turned over and began to think once more of Kay's hands, her laughter, and her blue eyes. Lee sighed as she silently acknowledged that she didn't want to dismiss Kay from her thoughts and unfettered her imagination. She felt Kay's kiss, her touch, her passion as Lee let her own hands answer her body's needs. Her sleep that night was deep and seemingly dreamless.

The morning went surprisingly quickly for Lee and she was barely ready when Kay's Jeep pulled up to the house. She met Kay on the porch with a happy grin and was delighted when it was returned. The drive down to the river was shortened by Kay's knowledge of the road and their laughter.

Kay pulled over onto the road's shoulder, then picked up her towel and a net full of beer cans. Lee slipped off her shorts and top, revealing her brown Speedo bathing suit.

"I just swim in my cutoffs," Kay explained. "Come on, I'll show you where the deep spots are."

They walked down to the river's edge and hung their towels on tree branches. Kay walked on in without a pause, carrying her net of drinks, so Lee followed and was unprepared for the shock of the water. Luckily the river deepened gradually so she had time to adjust. They were about waist deep when Kay pointed ahead a

few yards. "There, just past that boulder it gets nice
and deep. Are you ready to swim yet? I forgot to warn
you about how cold it would be."

"Let's go," Lee laughed and plunged ahead. She dove
into the deeper water and felt the chilling shock of it
covering her whole body. She came up sputtering, then
dove again. This time the water felt like a blessing as it
streamed around her heated body. Lee swam for some
time, enjoying the freedom the water gave her.

Finally tired, she swam back to the big boulder and
stood up in the shallow water. Lee looked around and
spotted Kay lounging half-submerged on some rocks in
the middle of the river. Kay gestured to Lee, inviting
her to join her.

Lee walked slowly through the water, enjoying the
picture of Kay leaning against the rocks. Kay's upper
body was covered with only a soaked, white muscle
shirt, and her tanned tapering legs stretched out in
front of her, visible through the clear water. Lee felt as
if she were walking toward a mirage as Kay smiled
invitingly up at her.

Lee sat carefully next to Kay and leaned back against
a hot, bare rock. She felt Kay's arm around her
shoulders and found it more comfortable to lean back
that way. That small gesture pleased her out of all
proportion.

"That suit looks great on you," Kay said as they sat
idly in the sun. "I can't wear browns or tans, but it
looks super on you."

"Thanks. I was admiring your muscle shirt."

Kay laughed. "It leaves little to the imagination, I
guess."

"Exactly."

"Here, I have to move my arm, it's asleep already.
Why don't you just lean on my shoulder? It'll be more
comfortable."

Lee complied, wondering at Kay's easy acceptance of
her touch. They sat quietly looking up river, as the

strong current ran into them, pulled at their legs, then moved on. Kay moved slightly, readjusting her seat and then rested her hand on Lee's thigh.

"I've always thought this was the perfect spot on a day like this. Just sitting here watching the river, talking and drinking. Want an extra light beer? It's as close as Dave's Carry Out comes to sparkling water."

"Sounds perfect."

Kay pulled in her net and fished out two cans. She handed Lee a beer and then resettled herself with her hand back on Lee's thigh. Lee enjoyed the cold beer and Kay's touch. She sat with eyes closed fantasizing about making love in the river when Kay spoke again.

"I'm glad you're back, Lee. It feels good to be together again on the mountain. How long will you stay?"

"I don't know for sure. At least the summer. There's really no reason for me to go back to Ohio. If I found a job here, I'd probably stay. But I don't know where I'd find a job."

"You might find something in Maryville or Sweetwater, but I suppose Knoxville is the best bet."

"Probably, but I'm not sure Knoxville is much different from any other city. For me, I mean."

"Sure," Kay agreed easily.

"Did you have a good trip yesterday?"

"Actually it was too hot and very boring. I had to go to drop off last month's meeting notes to the regular secretary. I took the minutes last time when she was gone. Our meeting's coming up soon, so Cathy wanted to see them."

"What meeting?"

"Oh, it's the Bi-County Health Services Coordination Committee. We meet once a month to try to keep track of county needs and problems. Care of the elderly is our biggest headache, although AIDS may be growing faster than we know."

"Are there many cases here?"

"No, not like the cities, not yet. It scares me when I think about it and the implications here."

"I can imagine. There must not be any extra funds."

"None at all," Kay affirmed. "There's no infrastructure to carry the caseload, to provide volunteer help, or long-term care. Our tax base is relatively small and not growing much larger at the moment. We don't have enough doctors or nurses or money for medication or anything else. Our hospice is just getting started, but at least we have one. I keep praying for time, but I know it's running out all across rural America. Our turn will come all too soon."

They fell silent again as they watched the mesmerizing movement of the river. The water's surface reflected the brilliant blue sky and the greens and browns of the overhanging trees. The water shimmered under the sun with incredible intensity. The only variation was the gray rocks and the ripples around them. A water snake skimmed across the sparkling surface, passing near their perch. Lee was relieved as it continued to swim with the current down the river without a pause.

"Did you visit your friends in Madisonville?" Lee asked.

"Yeah, I saw Toni and Margarette, but Terry was in Knoxville. I guess she's planning to move back there to be with her lover. She always was a city person."

That's one question answered, Lee thought.

The lazy afternoon continued with more beer and an occasional swim to keep cool.

"Kay, do you remember our last year here together, when we were fourteen?" Lee asked, as they sat once more on the rocks.

"Of course. I've been reminiscing a lot since you came to see me."

"After the ride and what I saw by the chimney, I've been remembering, too. Were we really that close, or was it just our first love?"

"Both I think." Kay hesitated, then continued. "I was thinking about that, too, as I drove yesterday. I remembered how we just knew things and felt things together. How I wanted to always be with you. It was probably a good thing we never became lovers."

"Why?"

"Well, besides being crushed when you left in September, I think it would have brought down too many barriers. I think between any lovers there's a bond that builds, linking them psychically. Touching, loving, trusting, strengthens that bond. We're both receptive, and your gift might have made the bond between us too strong to break. All the barriers would have been gone for us at fourteen, and that would have been too soon. I didn't have a clue about myself then, and I needed to grow. It was best that we both left."

"Are you glad I'm back?"

"Very." Kay's face still looked upstream.

"What about those barriers that you need?"

"Needed." Kay emphasized the past tense. She turned and looked directly into Lee's eyes. "Anytime you'd like to break through those barriers just let me know."

Kay's face broke into a grin and she winked, relieving the intensity of the moment. Lee smiled back, then leaned against Kay's shoulder and relaxed in the sun. Kay's hand gently caressed her thigh, and Lee felt her body's pleasure with Kay's touch.

"How about tonight?" Lee fought to keep her voice light.

"Shit! Why does this have to happen?" Kay's voice held a tinge of amusement along with the irritation. Her eyes held Lee's with their honest candor. "You're not going to believe this, but I have to go to Knoxville tonight. I have a massage class. I've been going for three months and tonight is our final. If I don't go, I'll have to start over."

"When will you get back?"

"Late. Probably after midnight."

"Well, I guess I better give you a raincheck then. How about tomorrow night?" Lee felt herself on the edge of laughter as Kay's face filled with frank pleasure and delight.

"Perfect."

Lee leaned forward and kissed Kay quickly. Kay laughed aloud. "Watch out, the neighbors mustn't know," she teased.

Lee joined in the laughter. Both women relaxed, their bodies touching casually. They talked and flirted in a comfortable fashion, allowing time to slip by like the river water about them.

♌ ♌ ♌

Kay dropped Lee off about five. She turned down Lee's supper invitation, but took the time to kiss Lee properly. Lee felt deserted as Kay drove away. That feeling caused as much concern for Lee as the kiss had caused excitement. She was on a seesaw, always up or down but never level.

Kay called later in the evening from Knoxville. She proposed another trail ride in the morning at seven. Lee agreed but demanded a romantic view as their goal. Kay guaranteed it with a laugh and said good night after Lee wished her luck on her test.

That night Lee slept restlessly, her mind troubled by her growing attraction to Kay and the fear of what that might mean. In the early morning, hours the air cooled and Lee slept deeply, undisturbed.

About four-thirty, she awoke, drank some milk, and fell back asleep, not worried about dreams or the future. She suddenly found herself in the midst of a realistic dream, once more riding Tellico. She was on the path to the Holt farm, Lee realized. Then she rode into the clearing, where she saw only Kay sitting on the old stump. There was no house or barn, or even a sign that they had ever existed. A full moon was rising over Kay's shoulder, dimming the bright canopy of stars. Lee got off Tellico and walked toward Kay, glad to see her waiting there. As Lee got closer to Kay, she saw that she wore what looked like a black, monk's robe. The white rope that served as a belt hung unused and the hood was thrown back. The robe was wrapped around Kay loosely, with only her crossed arms holding the sides together. The moon shone down on Kay's hair, reflecting off the silver strand tucked behind one ear. The rest of her hair was untied and moved freely in the gentle night breeze.

Kay smiled at Lee without any reservation. "I've been waiting for you. I'm glad you've come. Come here." She beckoned to Lee, although she remained seated on the stump.

Lee stopped, feeling uneasy. She knew that Tellico was gone, that he couldn't walk here. She looked behind Kay at the high wall of bushes that reminded her of the tall hedges in a maze. Lee turned around slowly, realizing she was in a circle of bushes with no way in or out. The inner area was covered with long, soft grass. The stump and Kay were at the center.

Lee turned back to Kay, wanting to ask what had happened. Kay smiled again and said. "Come here."

Still Lee stood, undecided what to do. Kay chuckled, dropped her hands, and jumped off the stump. The robe blew back then, surprisingly, opened in front, and seemed to flow away from Kay's body. She stood there, hair and robe moving in the wind, her body naked in the moonlight.

Kay extended her arms and called, "Come here."

Lee stood still and looked one more time for an opening in the hedges. She was almost afraid to look back at Kay, but the image in the moonlight was too beautiful to ignore.

Kay spoke gently again. "Come here, Leah. Don't you know yet that the only way out is through me? Come here, and love me."

Lee walked into those waiting arms and felt them tighten around her. Kay's lips met hers, promising unlimited passion. Kay pulled back a moment, smiled into Lee's eyes and spoke.

"You are so beautiful in the moonlight. Lie down with me."

Lee was lying beside Kay, feeling Kay's lips burning her throat and ears. She felt Kay's hands caressing her inner thighs, searching for her heat. Then all of time stopped as Kay's fingers slipped inside her. Kay held her, moving as if Lee's body were her own. Lee's pleasure grew until it seemed beyond reality; then waves of pure joy broke over her and seemed to continue forever.

Lee turned to Kay, aware now of what she must do. "I want to make love to you, to feel as you do and give it back again," she whispered.

Kay reached up for her as Lee lowered herself onto Kay's body. She kissed Kay's lips and then let the barriers go.

Suddenly Kay's body was hers. Kay's need burned inside Lee. Her ache led Lee's fingers, directed her kisses, drove her tongue in its darting explorations.

Lee felt her own desire and how her own body touched Kay's. But there in her mind were Kay's feelings as well. Every bit of Kay's response to her own slightest touch was present in Lee's thoughts. She let the independent sensory images mingle and mix in her mind. Then as they played together and overlapped, she shared her gift with Kay.

Their lovemaking was like a symphony, sometimes slow and heavy; then it tripped along, returning eventually to a central theme. They loved together, out of body, out of time, out of place. When the climax came, Lee fell through to nothingness. Only Kay was there, all about her, and the waves of pulsing light their love had made.

Lee awoke slowly and looked around, feeling entirely disoriented. Something momentous had happened, but what? The dream came back gradually, in bits and pieces at first, then every scene. Lee was overwhelmed.

Lee tried to understand what had happened. The barriers between her and Kay had slipped away. But then? How could anyone feel another, experiencing two bodies at once? How had that shared feeling gone back to Kay?

Lee stopped, feeling fear rise. This was crazy. Just like the dreams and drunken, stoned wanderings her mind had made up in Ohio were crazy. Kay couldn't possibly have meant this when they talked yesterday. No one could be expected to trust that much, reach out that much, and then give in to it that way. It was just impossible. How would she ever find herself again?

Lee hugged herself, letting the feel of her own body relieve her fears. She glanced at the clock and realized it was time to get up. She'd have to hurry if she was going to be at Kay's by seven.

In the rush of breakfast and getting Tellico ready, Lee pushed her dream away. It seemed even more unreal during the mundane, everyday chores of her world. Lee tried to dismiss it entirely, but through the day it continued to come to mind, forcing her to reconsider.

Chapter 6

It was about ten of seven in the morning when Lee rode her horse into the Holt farm clearing. Lee had noticed the caw of the crows as she came through the cemetery, so she was not surprised to have Kay meet her halfway to the barn.

"Why don't you tie him in that same stall? I just got started on lunch, so it'll be a while. Come on up and you can make the sandwiches." Kay turned back to the house.

Lee tied up Tellico and made him comfortable. Then she headed back to the house, very aware of her aches and pains. Too much riding, too soon, she thought. She walked into the kitchen and found Kay washing some apples. Kay turned, wiped her hands on a towel, and gave Lee a welcoming hug and kissed her cheek. Lee was surprised at her own reticence. Then she recovered and returned the hug wholeheartedly. She pushed the memory of her dream firmly away.

Kay turned back to the sink and pointed to the refrigerator. "The bread and chicken are in the frig. I like mayonnaise, sprouts, and cheese. There's tomatoes, too, but they're not great."

"Okay."

Lee started pulling everything out and spreading out the bread. "One or two, Kay?"

"Better make it two."

Just then the phone rang. Kay answered after a couple rings.

"Hi, Doris—what? Slow down, okay? Its nose is showing and no legs? Okay, now listen. Get her up and walking no matter what. I'll be there in about five minutes."

Lee had turned and listened, wondering what the problem was. Watching Kay's face, Lee knew that their ride would be delayed. She had everything back inside the refrigerator by the time Kay hung up the phone.

Kay turned and explained with a tight, worried smile. "If you want to volunteer, I'm going to need an extra hand or two. We've got a mare and foal in trouble."

Lee nodded and waited for instructions.

"Go on out to the Jeep and get it started. Pump it first. The keys are on a hook by the front door. I'll be right there."

Kay turned and went to her workroom. Lee went to the front door, grabbed the keys, and headed for the Jeep as fast as she could. She was cursing her sore legs by the time she reached the car.

Kay was right: the Jeep was temperamental. But Lee got it idling and moved into the other seat as Kay ran up. "Where are we going?" Lee asked as Kay put the Jeep in gear.

"McMurphy's, just above you on Rafter Road. We're taking a short cut, so hold on; it'll get bouncy," Kay answered as she turned up past the cemetery on the dirt road and continued along it.

Lee was glad for the warning when she saw the road they were turning on. It was the other branch of the old logging road, used mostly by hunters now. It was rutted and rocky in places and full of shifting gravel in others. They even drove through a small creek that was about six inches deep. It would have been a beautiful ride in the early morning if it had been a bit slower.

In four minutes they were back on Rafter Road and in McMurphy's barnyard. Kay grabbed her case of supplies and ran for the barn with Lee trailing her.

Lee made it to the barn as Kay and Doris McMurphy were leading the mare out. They took her up behind the barn where there was a steep hill.

"Put her head downhill, Doris," Kay said. "That'll put the baby back down in the birth canal and give us a chance to get those legs out."

Kay turned to Lee and explained as she put on a long sterile plastic glove that extended to her arm pit. "The foal presented with its head first and its front legs folded back underneath it. Usually they kind of dive out of the mare, front legs first, with their head tucked down between the legs. I have to go inside and find the feet and straighten the legs out.

"Put that KY all over this glove. Then you'll have to hold her tail out of the way. If she tries to lay down, hold her tail up in the air and try to keep her up. Doris, keep her head up if she tries to go down."

"I'll try, Kay," Doris answered.

Lee nodded her understanding and watched in fascination as Kay put her arm slowly inside the dilated mare. Kay's face was tense, her jaw clenched, as she forced her arm deep into the mare. Lee realized Kay was using incredible strength to push against the mare's strong birth contractions. Kay broke into a sweat yet continued to move deeper inside the mare until nearly her entire arm was immersed. Lee saw her shoulder and chest muscles strain as she began to move laterally. Kay moved carefully, gently searching for one of the front feet.

Lee watched, feeling helpless. "I wish I could help you feel it somehow," she said to Kay.

Kay nodded, her attention focused entirely inside the mare.

Suddenly Lee was the mare. She knew her panic, exhaustion, pain, and fear. She felt the mare's knowledge that her baby was in trouble and that it could mean death for one or both of them. She could feel Kay's arm moving away from the foal's foot.

"Move about three inches to your left and stretch out your fingers." Lee's voice had the certainty of truth.

Kay frowned and then adjusted her hand. She smiled a little. "Found one. Now we just got to straighten it out. I have to cup my hand around the hoof, so momma doesn't get hurt."

Kay's face was a study in determined patience. She gradually drew her arm out, timing her movements to coincide with the mare's strong contractions. The foal's small front hoof was visible between the outer lips of the mare's vulva once Kay's arm was free. Kay turned to Lee. Sweat dripped off her forehead, and her T-shirt was plastered to her body by a smelly mix of blood, sweat, and horse manure.

"More KY. We still have the left one to find. It's hard work. Mares are even more muscular internally than cows."

"I've never seen anything like this."

"I've never done it by myself, and I'm glad for any help, but don't tell Doris," Kay admitted in an undertone and winked. "Doing fine Doris. One leg's out and I think I felt the other," she said with a raised voice.

Doris just nodded. Her face was pale and tired.

Kay slowly put her arm inside the mare again. Her muscular arm and shoulder strained. This time it seemed to go more quickly, Lee thought. Kay smiled in triumph as she pulled the other front leg forward.

"That's it. Walk her back to her stall Doris and let's get this foal born."

They followed the mare back to the barn and waited outside. Doris stayed with the mare, talking to her in a low voice while the horse settled a bit and laid down again.

"Do you think the foal will be all right?" Lee asked.

"Probably, but it might have contracted tendons, and that'll be a problem. Doris has waited a long time for this baby. She'll help it along if it needs it," Kay answered. She was half listening to the sounds in the barn as she talked. Then her blue eyes caught Lee's gaze. "Lee, how did you know where the foal's foot was?"

"I don't know. It just seemed right. I've seen mares foal before, but I never saw a problem birth. Does it happen often?" Lee continued, trying to draw Kay away from the thought of Lee's intervention.

"No. Probably 95 percent of the mares I've seen deliver with no problems at all. In fact, it goes a lot smoother if they are left alone. But for a few cases it's good if someone is at least keeping track of what's going on. Doris probably saved both her mare and her foal this morning." Kay turned and smiled as Doris came back out.

"She's down and it's coming, Kay, just like it should. Thank you."

"Sure. We'll stay to check the baby," Kay reassured her. "You better go back in and talk to Molly. Encourage her. She's probably real tired and sore."

Kay turned back to Lee. "I'm afraid we won't get to ride today. It'll probably take an hour at least before that baby's up, if then."

"That's okay," Lee said with a smile. "This will make a great story."

Kay laughed quietly. "I guess I'd better watch myself if my actions are going to be written down for posterity."

"You bet," Lee joked. "I'll call it Dyke in the Wilderness or maybe Lesbian Herbal Doctor."

"I'd rather be called a witch," Kay said with a grin, her blue eyes twinkling.

"You are rather bewitching," Lee teased.

"Oh?" Kay asked, her eyebrows arched inquiringly. "Are you under my spell already?"

Caught by the intensity of Kay's look, Lee felt her face turning red. She was saved from replying by Doris' timely reappearance.

"Come on in, you two. Molly's got a baby."

Lee felt elated. They went inside to find Molly still lying down but her head was turned, looking at her new foal. The loving fervor of her look made Lee swallow hard. The mare gave a low, gentle nicker; the foal bobbed its head in answer and then gave a low, throaty whinny.

ॐ ॐ ॐ

It was almost two hours before they drove back to Kay's farm. Kay had checked the foal and announced it was a boy. The placenta was checked as well. The colt's tendons were slightly contracted, so Kay told Doris to call the vet about treatment. She also showed her a massage to use on the baby's legs.

As they got into the Jeep, Kay looked at her clothes and grimaced.

"Well, I started out clean today. Maybe I should get some vet overalls like Doc Samuelson uses. Can you see me in khaki?"

Lee laughed. "No, just in old jeans and T-shirts. You just look like you've been busy saving the lives of a mare and foal. Don't worry; the blood won't stain anything.

"Let's go back the way we came," Lee added as Kay put the Jeep in gear. "I'd like to take the scenic route again, but slower this time."

"Great." Kay nodded and turned down the old logging road. Kay took her time, pointing out what was left of an old log cabin and stopping by the stream to show Lee the tiny trout.

"How did you learn about treating horses?" Lee asked as they drove slowly toward the farm.

"Mostly from Grandma Dixie. I did work for a while as a vet's assistant in Oregon, but I couldn't stomach all of the job. Dixie showed me a more positive approach: using my own energy with the animal's, asking for their help. It works better for me."

Kay's words were carefully chosen. Lee got the feeling that too often Kay tried to communicate her ideas to people who didn't know animals. She knew how that felt herself.

"Do the local vets object to your practicing in their area? And what about the doctors?"

Kay smiled gently at Lee before she explained. "Things are a little different here. It's a long way to get medical help of any kind, so both patients and doctors are a bit more flexible. I'm very careful not to step on toes, and I often send people to vets or doctors. This way I can take care of the emergencies like today, or the chronic conditions that medical doctors never get to see around here. Money is always tight and everyone is very independent. It works out well."

Lee nodded, trying to imagine someone like Kay around Cleveland. It would probably never work.

They parked the Jeep by the cemetery and walked back to the house. The day was getting hot and muggy, and Lee's dirty clothes stuck to her.

"I think we both could use a nice, cold shower," Kay suggested. "Stay here, I'll get us towels and clean shirts." Lee waited on the porch, and Kay returned with an arm load of supplies.

"Follow me," she commanded.

"Where are we going?" Lee asked in concern as she noted the direction of Kay's stride.

"Oh Lee, you must remember the falls?" Kay turned to her, her face deeply disappointed.

"Well of course I do Kay," Lee said, a little exasperated. "But how do you expect me to climb down there?"

"Follow me, woman," Kay grinned. "There have been major improvements."

Lee followed Kay down the gap in the ridge and saw ahead of them steps cut into the steep hillside with wood rails in place.

"Grandma wanted to be able to enjoy it, too," Kay explained over her shoulder. "So I worked all one spring getting this done. I'm glad I have it for myself now."

Lee could hear the fast-flowing creek below them, but trees and underbrush still hid the falls. Finally they came around a big clump of laurel and just below them were the miniature falls.

The waterfall was only ten or twelve feet high. It cascaded down over rocks that had been cut back underneath the overhang so there was a ledge under the spray. All around the stream were big, smooth, gray rocks that were part of the creek bed during floods. Trees arched overhead, and soft, lacy ferns grew along the bank. Old leaves crunched underfoot, and dark green moss grew in patches on the rocks. As the sunlight streamed down into the tiny valley past the falls, it seemed to be filled with green and gold droplets. Even the air smelled green and wet.

Lee paused to look around and remember. She was astonished that this one place from her childhood was just as beautiful as her memories, and completely untouched. Kay had gone on to hang up the towels and clothes. She looked back at Lee and smiled at her enraptured expression.

"This is one of my most favorite places, too," Kay said with pleasure. "Come on, I've got to get cleaned up. These clothes are stinky."

"Go ahead. It'll take me a few minutes to climb over there," Lee answered.

"Okay."

Lee started to take off her clothes and fold them up. She looked up when she heard Kay sputter under the

cold water of the falls. Lee caught her breath, looking
at her friend standing naked under the tiny falls.

"Oh god, it's cold! My head is freezing," Kay shouted.
Lee laughed aloud, knowing that Kay's shouts helped
keep the intensely cold water bearable. She continued
to watch Kay as she took her own clothes off. She felt
her body stir, responding to the beautiful image before
her. So how did she handle this, feeling this need when
she was with Kay? How could she want anyone now,
when she felt so fearful, so isolated?

Lee walked close to the falls before she took off her
shoes. She felt unsure of how to keep her balance on
the wet rocks. Suddenly Kay was beside her, dripping
cold water on her hot skin.

"Do you need help?" she asked Lee matter-of-factly.

"Yes, I'm afraid so. My left leg's a little shorter, and
I'm not real good at balancing myself yet."

"What do you want me to do?"

"Just stay close," Lee requested, "in case I slip."

"Okay." Kay smiled tenderly. "That's a pretty good
assignment, considering."

Lee wrinkled her nose at Kay and then stepped under the spray of the falls. The cold made her hold her
breath; then she moaned. She could step backward just
enough to get out of the water and soap up. Stepping
into the spray wasn't as shocking this time, and the
soap quickly slipped off her body. Kay handed her the
shampoo, and Lee scrubbed it into her short hair. Back
under the falls Lee gritted her teeth, trying to get completely rinsed without turning to ice.

She took Kay's hand as she came out from under the
falls. Lee felt herself slip on the slick rocks, but both
of Kay's hands were around her quickly, holding her.
Kay steadied Lee, and Lee moved toward her. Lee
picked each step carefully, not looking up until their
bodies practically touched.

Lee glanced up into Kay's face and saw her concerned look. Lee smiled, looking at those marvelous

blue eyes and feeling her stomach twist because Kay
was so near. Kay's face changed from worry to an
intense, deep look that Lee remembered from twenty
years before. Kay's arms tightened and she bent to
kiss Lee.

It was a gentle hello kiss at first, tentative, asking.
Lee let herself respond, feeling Kay's warm body
against hers and the heat in herself. Kay pulled her
closer, and the kiss deepened. It felt wonderful, so Lee
let herself get lost in the feeling, lose track of time and
place.

Finally Kay drew back, her face a mixture of intense
happiness and withdrawal.

"I guess we better go sit down, huh?" Kay asked
tentatively, looking into Lee's eyes, still wondering if
everything was all right.

"Yes, I think so." Lee smiled at Kay and at the
huskiness of her own voice as she tried to answer.

They walked together over to the big beach towel
Kay had spread out. Lee sat down carefully and Kay
sat close beside her, one arm around Lee's shoulders.

"I'm sorry. That just sort of happened," Kay said,
half smiling, still unsure.

"Just like it did the last time we were here," Lee said
as she put a hand on Kay's knee. "It felt just as good
today, Kay, as it did then. And I'm a lot less scared."

She turned to look into Kay's face, meaning to continue but getting lost in those blue eyes.

Kay bent toward her again and kissed her. It was
tender and loving, and Lee leaned toward her almost
automatically. Kay's naked body felt silken against
hers. Lee was stirred by the touch of Kay's soft,
rounded breasts. Kay gently kissed her mouth and
nose, then her eyes. As Kay's lips traveled around her
neck to her ear, Lee realized that she had to say stop
soon, or her body was going to melt.

"Kay," Lee said, her voice very low. "Kay, I can't."

Kay stopped and pulled back, her eyes questioning, but trusting. "Why not, Leah? Is there somebody else?"

"No, nobody at all," Lee answered, and looked at Kay's face. Her look made Kay lean toward her and kiss her firmly on the mouth. Kay held onto her burying her face in Lee's blond hair.

"Why then? Tell me why," Kay murmured.

"I'm scared of me, Kay. It's been a horrible year in ways I don't think you can understand. I've pushed everyone away from me, and I wouldn't want to do that to you."

"You won't," Kay answered, kissing Lee's hair, her arms tightening.

"Listen to me, Kawi." Lee's voice made Kay stop and pull back away. She looked at Lee's face, seeing the pain and worry.

"Tell me, Leah."

"I don't want to hurt you. This place, these mountains are part of my dreams. You are part of my dreams. I don't want to screw up my dream-come-true by rushing it, rushing myself. Please, Kawi."

"Okay." Kay smiled crookedly. "I didn't think you remembered my real name."

"How could I forget Kawi, my blue-eyed deer?"

"Can I hold you then?" Kay asked, her eyes gentle and smiling.

"Sure. That would feel good."

They lay down together, and Kay wrapped her arms around Lee. Lee relaxed, feeling like she had finally found her home. She held Kay too and listened to the music of the falls. The falling water splashed rhythmically against the rocks in a minor key. Birds, insects, and the moving leaves added undertones to the sweet song.

After what seemed a long, long time Kay stirred. "We have to go up, Leah. We can eat and then I have to go to work. Maybe we can talk?"

"Okay."

They gathered up their towels after getting dressed, and made the climb back to the house. It was easy, thought Lee, with Kay's smiling, warm presence beside her.

Chapter 7

The two women sat across from each other, finishing the lunch that had been planned for their trail ride. An easy silence lay between them as they ate, with the muted sounds of the mountain in the background. A crow cawed below, and Kay tilted her head listening.

"Someone coming?" Lee asked.

"No, I don't think so," Kay said, still listening.

"Sounds more like a dog or something."

"Are there dogs running loose up here?"

"A few, but they're usually pretty timid. Do you have a dog?" Kay asked.

"No, not yet. I always wanted a big dog, one that you could pat as you walk along. But I wouldn't want to get one until I was really settled."

"That makes sense." Kay paused, trying to gauge Lee's mood. "Lee, can we talk about what's happening between us?"

"Sure, but you go first." Lee said, suddenly shy.

"Well, I guess I'm surprised a little about how much I care, but I shouldn't be," Kay started out. "You were always special, the person who made summertime magic. I think I was always looking for you in other people—other women. When I heard you were back on the mountain, I started remembering and hoping it would be the same." Kay smiled a little.

"It isn't, of course," Kay continued, looking directly at Lee. "It's more now Lee, even more special. I want it to be more. I don't want to settle for a stolen kiss this time."

Lee looked up from her empty plate and was caught by Kay's intensity. She tried to explain what she felt.

"Kay, you're just as special to me. I remember I'd get so excited when summer came. I saved lists of things that happened to me during the year to share with you." She paused to gather her thoughts then went on. "When I saw you in town and then a few people told me to visit you, it felt like an old fantasy. These last few days it's been magic. You're everything I remember and much more. What's happening between us is special, Kay. I just want to go slow and make sure.

"I need to explain what's happened to me, why I'm so scared." Lee stopped, knowing it would be hard. Kay reached across the table to hold Lee's hand. Her warm touch was immediately reassuring.

"The accident was about a year ago. I was driving. Some idiot drove through a stop sign at fifty miles an hour. Mom died instantly, and I was pinned in the car for about an hour. It was horrible to be inside and not be able to do anything to help Mom or myself. I still dream about it."

Lee stopped, horror and sorrow constricting her throat. She glanced at Kay's sympathetic face and then looked away, unable to accept Kay's compassion without dissolving into tears. She began to speak once more by enforcing strict control on her emotions.

"I healed faster than the doctors expected and went back to work while I was still in physical therapy. But it didn't go well. I couldn't sleep. I'd dream about the accident or dying myself in some horrible way. Then I started dreaming that parts of my body were gone or that someone was going to attack me."

Kay squeezed her hand while Lee caught her breath. Lee began again, pain in her voice. "I went to a therapist and worked through some of it. But I still pulled away from everyone—my friends, relatives and my brother. I broke up with my lover because I couldn't share myself anymore. I was afraid I would hurt her somehow, destroy her along with myself.

"I started looking at my life and questioning everything: my career, my goals, my friends, even my clothes. I stopped trying new things, even though I was throwing all the old ones away. I'd only do old, safe, familiar things, things that Mom always agreed with. Finally, I couldn't stand it any more and ran back here."

"It was pretty brave to come here and leave it all behind," Kay observed, quietly offering support to combat the pain that was so visible on Lee's face.

"Not really," Lee countered. "This is a safe place for me, part of my childhood. The only chances I've taken are buying Tellico and finding you."

"And I've scared you to death?" Kay asked with a slight smile, but concern was in her eyes.

"No—well, yes, a little. But now that I've found you again, I don't want to mess it up." Lee looked at Kay, trying to smile.

"Kay, I wish the only problems were the accident and my fears and nightmares. But now there's more."

"This has something to do with today, doesn't it? It's why you were able to help me with the foal and why you didn't want to talk about it." Kay's eyes widened slightly. Concern and tenderness deepened her blue gaze.

"How did you guess?" Lee was perplexed.

"It felt right. So tell me, what's going on?" Kay encouraged.

"Well, it's like at the chimney, but different. More like the hawk. Do you remember the hawk?"

"Sure, you joined her in flight."

"I saw through her eyes, knew her thoughts, and felt her body, too," Lee added.

Kay nodded.

"It's started again, after all these years, just like when we were young. At first it only happened when I was drunk or stoned. That was fairly often then. After the accident, I straightened up my act, tried to stay sober. Then came the dreams and nightmares. I forgot the other, pushed it away. Then about four months ago, just when I was beginning to feel normal, it started again.

"This time it was different. I found myself in the body of a wino. Then I was an old, pain-racked woman who sat next to me on the bus. Then I was running around scared, hungry, and hurt because I was part of this poor lost dog."

"Was it always so depressing? Those sound like really negative experiences."

Lee nodded. "For the most part they were. But I remember thinking there was always an attitude of self-reliance, independence, and self-preservation in everyone. These people experienced a negative external life, yet at the core they sifted through it all and kept it balanced."

"I don't think I understand."

"I'm not sure I do either, except when I'm there with them," admitted Lee. "And I never know for sure just what is real and what is imagined. I've asked myself if it's some solipsistic vision that I've developed to protect or entertain myself. I've wondered if it's an infantile regression caused by Mom's death and I'm trying to return to the connected safety of the womb. But I can't be sure of anything, even my own theoretical explanations. I lose my boundaries, I lose myself, and I come back terribly afraid. I always feel that someday I'll be gone and that other being will still exist with me stuck inside."

"That would be enough to scare anyone. It's like a fear we all have to some extent when we fight to become our own person. I can't ever imagine relinquishing myself completely." Kay paused, then frowned. "I'll bet what I said yesterday, about bringing barriers down between us didn't reassure you much." At Lee's nod, she continued. "I'm sorry if it sounded negative to you. I always imagined you as an empath, sharing another's emotional, physical, and mental being without any negative side at all. It always intrigued me. When I was younger, I hoped you could teach it to me so I could use it with animals and children. So I'd be able to really know what was wrong instead of just making an educated guess."

"Well, that part works," Lee assured her. "Today I joined the mare almost by accident, and felt where the foal was. That's how I could tell you. I don't know if I could by choice, though."

"Maybe you could practice."

"Maybe. It still scares me some. I don't know the rules, how far I can go without problems. But I need to try. I'd rather be in control a bit more." Lee smiled wryly.

Kay chuckled. "You know when I was fourteen and fantasizing as often as possible, I used to wonder about making love." Seeing Lee's lopsided grin, Kay smiled and tried to clarify her thoughts. "I used to dream about making love to you. Then I'd ask myself how it would feel if your lover could read your mind, know what you felt, give you exactly what you needed. I guess that was in the back of my mind when I talked about barriers yesterday."

Lee was uncertain of what to say. Should she talk about her dream and admit why she was afraid to make love with Kay?

Kay had continued, not sensing Lee's quandary. "When I first made love to another woman, I decided

that was what my fantasies were really about. We knew
how to love each other because we were alike."

"Maybe." Lee's tone made Kay focus on her again.
Her face became inquisitive, so Lee responded.

"I dreamed about you last night, about us. We made
love and it was so different, so far beyond anything
I've ever felt. But it frightened me, Kay. At the end we
weren't even physically here anymore. I don't know
what happened, what it meant. All I know is it frightened me badly.

"You're too special to lose again because of some
nightmares or memories. That's why I want to go slow,
so I don't get scared and run away."

The phone rang and both of them jumped. Kay
looked annoyed, but got up to answer it. She listened
then her face became thoughtful, her attitude intent.
Lee realized how much Kay loved her work and suddenly found herself ardently proud of Kay's dedication.

"Don't worry John. We can stop it before it gets the
better of them. I'll be there in a half hour or so."

Kay hung up the phone and turned to Lee. "Sorry,
honey. Duty calls. John Rosemont has some baby pigs
that have the scours. It can be serious if it isn't caught
in time. I've got to pack a bag."

Lee nodded her understanding as she remembered
a foal that had developed a bad case of scours. The
diarrhea had dehydrated the baby so badly that its
whole system had been left vulnerable. That foal had
pulled through because of hours of work and unlimited antibiotics.

She got ready to leave, and Kay caught her at the
door. "What, no goodbye kiss?" Kay asked playfully.
She started to give Lee a gentle peck, but Lee wanted
more. She kissed her, bringing her entire body against
Kay's, letting her body say what had been left unsaid.
Kay responded, pressing Lee back against the door
jam, convincing Lee that she was melting inside.

Kay pulled back, smiling slightly. Her eyes made Lee
feel that she should reach out for Kay's body again.
But Lee willed herself to be reserved.

"Can I stop by after supper?" Kay asked, as her
hands remained on Lee's arms.

"Sure."

As Lee nodded emphatically, Kay kissed her again
passionately. They stood there, responding to their bodies' need to hold each other until reason returned.

Lee said goodbye and headed for the barn. She took
her time tacking up Tellico, and was both glad and
depressed as she heard Kay's Jeep drive away.

ᘯ ᘯ ᘯ

Lee rode home, talking to Tellico about her day. He
seemed pleased to have spent the day relaxing in a
stall, out of the bugs and enjoying hay.

That afternoon, Lee found her thoughts often on
Kay. She found herself thinking of Kay's face, her deep
blue eyes, the tone of her voice, the way her body
moved. Lee's body ached as she imagined Kay's touch
and how it would feel to explore Kay's beauty.

Lee pulled herself up short, reminding herself she
barely knew Kay, this Kay. Until the accident, Lee had
enjoyed easy short-lived relationships. She and her
friends had spent lots of nights at the bar, drinking,
dancing, and flirting. For Lee, jumping into bed had
been simple and fun, fulfilling in itself. Now she had a
feeling of restraint. She wanted more with Kay, but she
didn't know how to go about finding it. The afternoon
passed slowly. Lee kept hoping Kay would come early,
but suppertime came and she was still alone.

Lee had just finished her solitary meal and was
rinsing the dishes when she heard Kay's Jeep turn off
Rafter Road. She met Kay on the front porch steps.

"Let's go feed Tellico," Lee suggested. "Then we'll
have the rest of the evening together."

Kay was amenable, so they strolled slowly hand-in-hand to the barn. The warm, evening air was muggy, and the sun was still bright, although shadows were beginning to deepen. Lee was glad to have help throwing down a bale of hay and another of straw. They bedded Tellico's stall with straw while he munched his grain. Bits and pieces of straw clung to their arms, so they headed for the watering trough to splash off. When they were cooler and less itchy, Kay suggested a walk.

They ambled along the pasture fence and then over to the grape arbor. Lee was surprised that the walk was so much easier than her first survey of the farm. The grape arbor was thick with big, green leaves and the tiny, new grapes that looked like milky green marbles.

"Do you remember when we decided to make wine?" Kay chuckled. "We made a mess, but the juice was luscious. Your grandma decided to let us just make two bottles of wine. Whatever happened to them?"

"If I remember right, Grandma said they exploded down in the cellar. We'd put too much of something in I guess. She was mad because the wine stained a chair she was refinishing. I think she had to sand it off."

Kay laughed. "Our grandmas certainly put up with a lot from us. Do you remember when we were really little, seven or eight, and we decided to help Grandma mix herbal teas?"

"Yes, and she kicked us outside because we couldn't remember which one was catnip or spearmint."

They laughed together, remembering their embarrassed disappointment and Dixie Holt's blustering dismissal. As they grew quiet, Lee heard the gurgling chuckle of the spring up the hill and walked toward it without thinking.

She squatted beside the bubbling pool and watched the water well up out of the ground. Lee felt caught again in the magic of the water appearing from nowhere and sharing its life with all it touched.

She felt Kay's presence behind her.

"I'm always drawn to this place when I'm feeling lonely or upset. The summer after you left, when I was fifteen, I spent most of my time here sitting under that old maple, trying to understand why you were gone. Every time I came back I'd ask for you, but your grandma wouldn't say much." She felt Kay's hand on her shoulder.

"I wasn't writing much to Grandma Dixie. It all seemed too strange in California. I thought she'd never understand. Then I started coming out and I just assumed I had to keep that from her, too," Kay explained.

"Let's go back inside."

They walked back to the house, staying close to one another, letting their bodies touch occasionally. Back in-side Lee poured them each a drink of tea and then led Kay to the living room.

"I'd thought we could watch a video. How about *Desert Hearts?*

"That would be great. I've only seen it once in Knoxville, and that was a while ago."

Lee put the tape in her VCR and turned to go sit down. Kay was settled in an easy chair off to one side. Lee marched over, grabbed Kay's hand, and started to pull. "I'm not going to sit by myself. You get your butt over on the couch beside me."

Kay looked startled, and then laughed. "I was just trying to go slow," she protested. But she rose and moved to one side of the couch.

Lee settled beside her with a smug smile. "I said slow, not nonexistent."

She put one arm around Kay and kissed her cheek. Then they settled down to watch the movie. They had watched fifteen or twenty minutes when the phone rang.

"Damn, who can that be?" Lee asked herself, stopping the video and answering the phone.

Lee was surprised when her Aunt Grace said hello. Her aunt reminded her that the upcoming weekend was Memorial Day and extended an invitation for her to come to Knoxville for the family celebration. Lee gracefully declined, citing pressing work. Her aunt was disappointed but continued.

"Well dear, I thought it might make Tuesday easier for you. But I'll let your Uncle Steve explain."

Kay looked questioningly at Lee's surprised face, and Lee answered with a wink and a shrug.

"Hi, Uncle Steve."

"Hello, Lee. I've got wonderful news. I ran into Greg Meeks yesterday and we got to talking about you. He was delighted with that piece on Grandpa Brant. I guess there was quite a lot of reader response. When he heard you were planning to stay in the area, he asked if you needed a job. I said I wasn't sure, but I knew you were freelancing some. He got excited and said he needed to see you on Tuesday, because he has the perfect spot for you. I said I'd relay the message." Uncle Steve's voice sounded proud and pleased.

"Well, huh, this is a surprise. Did he give you an idea of what he had in mind?"

"Just that it was full-time under him in the county section. He wanted you to call his office tomorrow to confirm the Tuesday appointment. Do you want the number?"

"Sure, I guess so."

After writing down the number, thanking her uncle and saying goodbye, Lee sat by the phone, a little stunned.

"What's going on?" Kay asked.

"I'm going to Knoxville on Tuesday for a job interview." Kay looked as startled as Lee felt.

"A friend of my uncle's is an editor there and he wants to offer me a job."

"Are you going?"

"I don't know—I guess so. A job on a big city paper
was what I dreamed about in Cleveland. I shouldn't
pass it up, really." Lee faltered.

Kay was frowning slightly. Forcing a smile, she cautioned, "Just remember, Lee, you're not in Cleveland
any more. So think it over carefully, huh?"

Noticing Lee's confused reaction, Kay qualified her
statement. "I meant to say that you should do what
you want, not what you're supposed to." Kay moved
over and hugged Lee slightly as she sat by the phone.
"I don't want you to stay up here if it's wrong for you
either. But don't assume that the choices that are good
for your career are always the choices that are good
for you."

Lee nodded and hugged Kay back. It felt as if her old
reality had stepped between them, infringing on their
shared space. She hugged Kay harder, kissing her, hoping the touching would hold those old feelings at bay.
Kay's response was warm but suddenly more reserved.

After a minute or two Kay pulled away. "Let's watch
the rest of the movie."

"Okay."

They settled on the couch again and started the tape
again. Lee felt Kay's continued reserve and wished it
could be otherwise. During the love scenes, Lee played
with the thought of seducing her friend but discarded
the notion. She wished the desire the scene had trig-
gered was as easily dismissed.

By the movie's end, they were more at ease with
each other. Kay was obviously tired and made moves
to leave. Lee kissed her goodbye, then gave in to herself and hugged Kay to her. They held each other for
several minutes.

"You're right, you know," Kay whispered. "We both
need to go slow."

Lee nodded and let her go. Kay left quickly and Lee
went to bed alone.

Chapter 8

As Lee drove north on Interstate 75 toward
Knoxville, she thought about her Memorial Day weekend. She and Kay had spent time together on Saturday
and Sunday, but had carefully given each other space.
Lee had written all Saturday morning, and they had
spent both evenings apart.

They had taken time to decorate the graves of both
their families on Saturday afternoon. Lee had never par-
ticipated in this tradition nor understood why anyone
did. But this year, she enjoyed the feeling of continuity,
of belonging, as she put a potted flower on Grandpa
Brant's grave.

On Monday, Kay had taken Lee to an arts and crafts
show in a small town in the valley. Lee enjoyed looking
at the hand-thrown pottery, wood carvings, and quilts.
They stopped and listened to a quartet playing tradi-
tional bluegrass. Lee watched the old fiddle player in
fascination. His weathered face and gaunt body were
perfectly still, while his right foot patted time and his
fingers flew over the fiddle. The old man's face showed
no emotion. His eyes were glued to the guitar player
next to him, while they played "The Falls of Richmond"
faultlessly.

As the tune ended, the appreciative audience
clapped and whistled their enthusiasm. The quartet immediately began a jig that roused the crowd to partici-
pation. Hands clapped, feet stomped, and a voice in
the back called yee-haa. A small girl beside Lee lifted
her long skirt and began to clog dance as her proud
parents marked time. The couple finally fell in step
with their child. Their legs thumped the jig's rhythm as
surrounding onlookers applauded and laughed.
Lee felt Kay next to her, clapping her hands in time
with the music. Lee let her right foot tap along and focused her eyes on the guitar player as he followed the
pace of the fiddler. How did it feel to play the fiddle
like that? How did it feel to be totally immersed in the
music, to create such a beautiful sound?
Lee blinked and tried to readjust her vision. She was
still watching the guitar player's hands form the
chords, but she was suddenly only a foot away. She
heard each part of the quartet, understood the phras-
ing, and anticipated what was coming in the next few
bars. She could feel the fingers of her left hand moving
quickly and intricately, while her right hand moved
smoothly back and forth. She glanced down to see her
booted foot marking time.
"Lee, hey Lee," Kay spoke near her ear.
Lee felt Kay's hand on her shoulder. She blinked
again and turned to look at Kay. She felt a touch of vertigo and shook her head slightly, closing her eyes.
"Honey, are you okay? What's going on?" Kay's voice
was concerned. Lee opened her eyes and found Kay's
blue stare disconcertingly close.
"I'm okay, just dizzy."
"It's the heat. Let's go find something to drink," Kay
suggested. Lee nodded and they moved out of the
small crowd.
They found a lemonade stand, purchased two tall
drinks, and retreated to sit under the trees. The solid
trunk felt reassuring as Lee leaned against the tree. She

relaxed in the cool shade, trying not to focus on the bizarre experience of a few minutes before. She glanced idly at the grass that was somewhat thin in the shade of the big maple.

Lee noticed a big, black ant striving to move a dead beetle. She watched the struggle as the ant dragged its prize through the miniature forest. Lee smiled, remembering a 1950s horror movie about giant, radioactive ants attacking Los Angeles. She started to wonder how it felt to carry something half-again as big as her own body, when she stopped in panic.

"Shit! I can't do that," Lee said aloud.

"What?" Kay had a half-smile, half-questioning look.

"Nothing—just talking to myself."

Kay looked unconvinced but remained quiet. Lee bit her lower lip, wanting to explain, but unsure of just what had happened. She looked away, and the moment passed.

Lee bit her lip again, remembering. Why hadn't she said anything to Kay? Why didn't she want to talk about her experience? Why was she leaving so much unsaid?

It's not that I don't trust Kay, Lee told herself. Maybe the experience is just too new, too unknown, and our relationship is just as new. So many things seemed to be happening at once.

$\mathcal{S}$　$\mathcal{S}$　$\mathcal{S}$

Lee drove past the first Knoxville exit and thought of Aunt Grace. Her house was on Fort Louden Lake in the midst of the growing suburbs. Lee decided to stop for a quick visit in the afternoon if she had time.

She got off the interstate and drove into downtown Knoxville to the newspaper's offices. Lee was surprised to find the crowds of pedestrians and traffic of the city distracting. She felt tired and depressed, and asked herself why she had decided to drive into the city. The contrast between her quiet life on the mountain and the intensity and heat of the city left her cursing at the drivers around her to vent her frustration.

She finally found a parking space and sprinted for the newspaper building, arriving three minutes early. Just long enough to get presentable, Lee thought, looking for the nearest restroom.

When she presented herself at Greg Meeks's office, Lee was amazed to be ushered in almost immediately. He rose to meet her halfway across the room, introducing himself and gesturing to a plush chair. Meeks was a dark-haired man in his mid-forties, dressed casually but well. He seemed friendly, poised, relaxed, and obviously at ease with the demands of his job. He perched on the edge of his big, paper-strewn desk.

"I'm glad you could come by on such short notice. Your Uncle Steve said you were down for the summer and might be interested in relocating. I told him I'd love to get you on my staff. Do you think you might be interested?"

Lee floundered, momentarily caught off balance by Meeks's aggressive style. Surely he knew she needed more information to answer that question.

"Well, yes, Mr. Meeks."

"Greg."

"Yes, Greg, if it sounded like a good position, I think I would be interested."

Greg Meeks smiled and nodded confidently. "I think you'll like it. It's full time in the county coverage section. I'd want local color pieces, with lots of historical depth and interviews. A lot like your article on your grandfather, but with more background research. Between your local family ties and your experience in Ohio, it'll be a snap."

Greg paused, looking at Lee, waiting for a reaction.

Lee struggled once more. "Well, I don't know, Greg. I guess I haven't thought much beyond this summer. Of course, I always wanted a newspaper job, but I never thought it'd be thrown in my lap."

Greg smiled and shook his head. "My readers let me know that you should write for the paper more often, so I'm just showing good judgment to try to hire you. I can offer a good salary, benefits, and a great town to live in," Greg continued.

Lee listened, surprised that the salary level was a significant raise over her magazine position's. Greg talked about his editorial slant and about the paper in general. She felt somewhat dazed when he finally ended his pitch.

"Tell you what, Lee. Your uncle said you were here recuperating. Think it over for a few days; there's plenty of time. Get back with me in a couple of weeks." Lee nodded and he continued. "Do you have plans for lunch? No? Good! I'm all booked up, but Maggie Brown said she'd stand in for me. You'd be working together some, so she can really fill you in."

Greg reached awkwardly back for his phone, never leaving his perch on the desk's edge. After a few terse words, he was smiling again at Lee, asking whether she had any questions.

"No, not now, but I'm sure I'll come up with plenty."

"Well, Maggie will be able to answer them all. Probably be more unbiased than I am too." Greg smiled, as there was a knock at the door and Maggie Brown walked in, right on cue.

She walked across the office, all angles and legs, and stood in front of Greg, relaxed yet assured.

"What's up Greg?"

"Maggie, this is Lee Kirby. She did that humorous piece on her grandfather for the Sunday section. She may be taking Ray's place and working with you. Can you take her to lunch and answer her questions? On my tab, of course."

"Sure, I'd be glad to, Greg." Maggie's voice sounded bored and resigned. She turned to Lee, her body language equally unenthusiastic.

Lee rose and offered her hand. She looked into Maggie's fine-boned face, finding soft, green eyes, and no makeup, framed by short, light brown hair. She watched Maggie's face change as she sized Lee up. They shook hands and smiled cautiously, their eyes acknowledging silent acceptance of a new acquaintance.

"Hi, Lee. Come on, I know the perfect place for lunch."

Maggie's smile widened, and Lee thought she saw a quick wink.

She barely had time to say goodbye to Greg Meeks as Maggie strode out of the office. Maggie paused long enough to sign out. Then she ushered Lee to the elevator and out of the building. Once outside, she slowed down dramatically, suggesting they walk to the restaurant. Lee agreed with relief, feeling a need to catch her breath and reconsider her interview. As they walked the four blocks to the restaurant, Lee realized she had felt overwhelmed by Greg Meeks's racing interview and his clear assumption that she would accept his offer.

"Here we are," Maggie said, opening a door. Inviting smells wafted out, so Lee didn't hesitate. Maggie pointed to a corner table, and Lee quickly sat down. Lee looked about, aware that almost all the customers were women. On the walls were pictures of famous women, although Lee had to admit she recognized only a third. She did recognize the music as a piano piece by Margie Adam.

Turning to Maggie, Lee raised her eyebrow questioningly. "I've never been in a restaurant quite like this, so women-oriented. How did you find it?"

"I know the two women who own it. I come here for lunch when I need a break from the office. I thought you might appreciate it."

Maggie's smile widened as she watched Lee's confusion. She decided to explain.

"When you leaned forward to shake hands, your necklace swung forward too. I recognized your labrys."

Lee could feel the red creeping into her face as she stammered. "That's the first time it's ever given me away."

"I thought that was the whole idea," Maggie laughed.

"Yeah, but it's never happened until I came back down here."

"Back down? I thought Greg told me you were from Ohio."

"Part of me is. I spent half my childhood down here with my grandparents. I've been living in Cleveland, so I guess I'm technically from Ohio, but the mountains always feel like home."

"I know what you mean," Maggie nodded. "I came here from Indiana, but I love it here. I think Knoxville is great."

"How long have you lived here, Maggie?"

"Just over two years. The first three or four months were rough, until I made some connections with other lesbians. Now I really feel at home."

Maggie paused to sip her diet cola. Lee took a few moments to look around speculatively, wondering how many of the lunch customers were part of the Knoxville women's community.

"What's the women's community like?" Lee asked.

"Oh, I guess it's like any place that's a city of this size. There are several different groups, as well as the college students, and we all have different interests and priorities. We do get together for gay pride marches and concerts, but that's about it. Lots of new women pop up all the time, like you, so it stays interesting."

Lee took the time to finish her sandwich before quizzing Maggie further. "How do things go at work. Are you out? Are there good people to work with?"

"Yes, Greg's managed to hire a couple of good
writers. Ginny White in editing is a good friend. There
are even two other lesbians working at the paper. I'm
out to some people, but not everyone. It's not really a
problem. Everybody respects my privacy. But tell me,
what about you? How did you end up back in Tennessee?"

Lee started telling Maggie the abbreviated version,
but was quickly put at ease. Maggie laughed a lot and
asked direct, intelligent questions. At the same time, it
was obvious that she really was interested in Lee. They
soon were deeply involved in conversation, pausing
only briefly to eat dessert.

When Maggie checked the time she groaned. "It's
almost two! I can't believe it." She shook her head, and
then turned to Lee. "Are you going to stick around
tonight? We could eat out and go to the bar. There'd
be plenty of dancing room tonight."

Lee hesitated only a moment. She was very aware of
Maggie's dancing green eyes and vibrant intensity.

"Sure, I'd love to stay, but not real late. It's a long
drive back."

Maggie grinned. "Why don't we meet at Nick's about
seven? It's at the corner of South and Grand. You like
Greek food don't you?"

"Sure."

"See you then. I've got to run, or Greg will skin me.
Order more if you want. I'll charge it on the way out.
Bye." Maggie smiled and was off.

Lee sat for several minutes wondering about the
whirlwind she seemed caught in. Maggie had been so
vibrant, so intensely there, then gone. It was a little
like riding an express elevator. But she had certainly
left Lee feeling excited and alive.

Lee decided to go to Aunt Grace's house for a quick
visit. Walking toward her car, she felt herself caught in
the city's rhythm. It made her feel a little high as she
walked purposefully along. She had missed this feeling

for more than a year, Lee suddenly realized. The intensity, quickness, and power of the city was almost intoxicating. Lee looked at the people walking hurriedly around her on their way to unknown destinations. They were all so contained, so self-oriented that they never really saw each other. How did it feel to be a young businessman, like that fellow in the gray pin-stripe, Lee wondered. How does it feel to be so full of one's self and positive about the future? Lee knew she was experimenting. But she felt no answering disorientation, no feeling of otherness or joining with the well-dressed young stranger. He continued down the block to a bank and disappeared inside. Lee was left wondering why his inner vision, unlike the old fiddler's, was closed to her.

Suddenly a memory flashed before her. It was a picture of herself two years before, on her way to interview a sponsor of the Cleveland Symphony. She was elegantly turned out, looking confident, walking downtown in Cleveland toward a tall office building. The parallel was clear, Lee admitted. She knew how that young man felt, how he talked, what he wanted ten years from now. She had already lived that life and had chosen to walk away from it.

Lee's steps hesitated, her thoughts jumbled, and she felt someone jostle her arm. "I'm sorry," Lee apologized quickly, and looked toward the offended party.

"That's all right, deary. I'm always bumping people. Everybody's just too much in a hurry these days," the old, bent, white-haired woman said.

Lee smiled at her and was rewarded with a gentle smile in return. The woman's eyes looked blurred and distorted behind heavy corrective lenses. But Lee saw the old woman's glance was as kind and knowing as any she had ever seen.

For ten seconds, she looked back at herself, an attractive blond woman with a gentle face and smile.

She felt the heavy glasses on her nose, the concentra-
tion it took to use their lenses for corrected vision and
the loss of peripheral vision altogether. She knew the
ache of arthritis in the hands holding the shopping
bag, the pinch of cheap, worn-thin shoes, and the con-
striction of the heavy corset around her middle. She
also felt the surprised warmth at being acknowledged
and treated kindly by a stranger on the city streets.

Back in herself Lee refocused on that sweet, old face.
"Do you need help with your bag?"

"No dear. I'm just going to the bus stop, right over
there. I'm fine, but thank you for asking." The white-
haired woman nodded and was on her way. Lee continued to her car, thinking hard about what she had just
experienced.

At Aunt Grace's, no one was home, so Lee walked
out toward the dock where she found a lawn chair. Lee
sat watching the muddy brown water of Ft. Louden
Lake and thinking about the future. Here was a perfect
job in a wonderful town, practically presented on a
platter. She could be near family, friends, and Kay. And
there's Maggie too, Lee added with a smile.

So, why didn't I tell Greg yes immediately? Why am I
feeling like there's a hitch somewhere? Mom would
have been delighted, and so would I a year ago. Now, I
keep asking what's wrong, although nothing seems to
be. Am I just afraid to take a chance? Or is there a
more valid reason?

Kay's smiling face formed in Lee's mind, and she
winced. Yes, she was afraid of losing Kay. How could
she live in the city and maintain that relationship? But
why not, Lee reasoned. They could see each other on
the weekends. They'd share lots of time together, and
they already had a firm foundation to work with. Why
not?

Lee took another tack, wondering about this strange
mental ability that was resurfacing. It seemed to be
growing easier, yet had boundaries she didn't

understand. How did it fit into her life? Would it
continue if she returned to city life? Was it part of
her future too?

Aunt Grace's voice interrupted her reverie. "Lee, are
you here?"

"Down here, Aunt Grace. I'll be right up."

Lee spent the next few hours with Aunt Grace and
Uncle Steve. They had fun swapping stories about the
mountain and the rest of the family. They both remembered Kay and were intrigued by her decision to return
to the mountain. Lee remained purposefully vague
when they asked about her interview and whether she
planned to stay in Knoxville. She also took time to call
her grandmother and invite her to visit Lee on the
mountain.

♌ ♌ ♌

Lee felt surprisingly unenthusiastic about leaving at
six-thirty to head back and meet Maggie. She found herself reluctant to drive back downtown. Lee didn't understand her feelings of uneasiness and disquiet, and she
pushed them away. But she couldn't ignore the dirt
and smell of the city, and the car exhaust that made
her choke.

She located Nick's restaurant easily and was pleased
to find Maggie waiting. They had a wonderful dinner,
sampling various Greek specialties, sharing their orders
with each other. They talked and joked like old friends,
and Lee forgot her uneasiness. Lee even tried Ouzo,
but despite Maggie's urging, switched to her usual wine
after one small taste.

It was still early, so Maggie took Lee on a guided
tour of the town. Lee was surprised at how much had
changed, how much new growth there was, yet she recognized a few buildings.

They reached the bar after ten. Lee was glad the
crowd was small. She was nervous about dancing

again, and just the presence of other people seemed a
little irritating.

Maggie led her to a small table tucked away from
the crowd. They could talk if they sat close. Lee found
herself drinking soda just to give her hands something
to do. She was surprised by how much the cigarette
smoke bothered her now. Maggie continued to talk,
telling Lee about some of the women at the bar. Lee
found herself laughing and enjoying the often ribald
stories.

They danced several times. Lee enjoyed it tremen-
dously after she stopped worrying about her balance.
She declined to slow dance until a favorite tune played.
Then she found herself dancing in Maggie's tightening
arms.

Maggie looked directly at Lee, her green eyes asking.
She pulled Lee close, their bodies moving together to
the music. Lee had a sense of déjà vu; then she realized that it was just a night like hundreds of others
spent in Cleveland.

Lee was very aware that Maggie wasn't Kay; her body
felt so angular, moved so differently. But Lee also felt
her own body respond to Maggie's closeness with a
warmth that surprised her. She tightened her hold unthinkingly, responding to the warmth. She felt Maggie
relax. They moved together easily, sensually, enjoying
the dance.

It was almost one when Maggie took Lee back to
Nick's to pick up her car. They were both a little tipsy
and more than a little intrigued with each other. They
sat together in Maggie's car while Lee went through the
motions of saying good night. Lee glanced into Maggie's eyes, surprised to find poorly masked desire there.

What is she feeling? What does she see when she
looks at me that way, Lee asked herself. For a few seconds, Lee found herself looking through Maggie's eyes
back toward her own face. She saw a blond woman
with a fresh, open face, who seemed entranced with

the person beside her. She felt Maggie's body, aching
for a touch. She knew Maggie's mind that played with
erotic images of the two of them, yet warned her to
stay cool, be careful, don't want too much.
Lee gazed back at Maggie from her own eyes again.
She still felt the memory of Maggie's need, and it
added to her own. She leaned forward pulling Maggie
to her and kissed her deeply. She let her hands move
down Maggie's back, caressing, and promising. They
broke apart, both surprised. Then Maggie pulled Lee
close again, kissing her hungrily.
    Lee felt the growing heat in her body and knew Mag-
gie's response like her own. She realized suddenly that
she was feeling not only her own arousal but Maggie's
as well. That doubled intensity was drawing her to Maggie. It would be so easy, Lee thought, to use those feelings, build on that inner knowledge, to reach a sexual
ecstasy neither had experienced before.
    Her body was already searching, reaching out, when
Lee heard an inner voice question what was happening.
Was this fair to either of them? Should she continue
this game, knowing its intensity would not be limited
to only their shared sexual experience? It would encompass everything they did together, overshadowing it all.
Was that fair to Maggie or herself, when they barely
knew each other?
    Lee pulled away gently. Holding Maggie, kissing her
hair, she felt both of their hearts slow, their breathing
quiet. She didn't want access to Maggie's body and
mind anymore, and she was not surprised to feel that
input suddenly end. She was just Lee again, holding
someone dear who had suddenly appeared in her life.
    After a few minutes, Lee cleared her throat. "Maggie,
I'm sorry. I guess I got a little carried away. That's not
my usual style, at least not lately. Scared myself, too."
    "It scared me too." Maggie's voice was low as she
leaned against Lee's shoulder. "I'm usually very reserved. For some reason I let myself step beyond the

limits I usually impose on myself. It was exciting and
frightening. I'm not sure what's going on, but I'd like to
see you again. Will I?"
    At the last word, Maggie drew back to gaze at Lee
with a look of tender questioning.
    "Yes, you will. That's a promise." Lee was emphatic.
"I'll call. I have to come back to see Greg later next
week. I'll let you know when."
    Maggie nodded, looking steadily at Lee. There were
dozens of unasked questions between them, but she
seemed content to leave them unsaid.
    Lee smiled and gently squeezed Maggie's hand. "I've
got to go."
    Maggie nodded. "Somebody waiting?"
    "Yes. But I'm not sure what's happening between us
either." Listening to herself, Lee realized that was a
half-truth.
    "You'd better hit the road, Lee. It'll be two-thirty
before you get home. Be careful, huh?" Maggie leaned
toward her, bestowing a gentle goodbye kiss.
    Lee drove carefully away, her mind in turmoil. What
had happened tonight? Who was Maggie? What had she
felt between them? Was it anything at all except a
reflection of her own sexual desire? She knew immediately that it was more than just imagination that had
allowed her to feel part of Maggie's response; something much more.
    Lee thought of the circling hawk and the old fiddler.
Then there was the old woman at the bus stop. Perhaps she needed to talk this out. Something more was
going on than just flights of fantasy. She knew Kay be-
lieved that, and Lee was almost certain herself. They
needed to talk about it together.
    Lee's mind played with ideas all the way home,
slipping easily from one idea to another. She didn't let
any idea stay in her mind for long or allow the memory of Maggie's lips on hers to gain hold again in her
imagination.

Chapter 9

Lee awoke with a pounding headache. She rolled over trying to remember why she felt so bad. Why did this feel like a hangover?

"Oh, god. I only had one glass of wine at supper," Lee moaned, as she began to remember the night before.

"Why am I awake?" she asked herself, taking a peek at her clock. It was seven-thirty, the time she usually got up, fed Tellico, and started her day. She drew the sheet back over herself trying to ignore the morning. In the distance she heard Tellico whinny, demanding his morning grain.

"Just half an hour more, please," Lee said, closing her eyes firmly, ignoring another loud neigh. She didn't let thoughts of her Knoxville visit intrude, using a well-worn fantasy to carry herself off to sleep.

About eight-fifteen, the sound of Kay's Jeep intruded into Lee's light doze. In a sleepy haze, Lee tried to understand why Kay was there so early. She finally remembered Kay had promised to feed Tellico the night before and again this morning. Lee was awake enough to hope Kay didn't drive up to the house.

As the sound of Kay's Jeep came closer, Lee forced herself out of bed. She thought briefly of faking sleep, but knew that was an open invitation to Kay's early morning good spirits.

"All I need with this headache is someone jumping into bed," Lee grumbled, as she pulled on a T-shirt.

Kay opened the back door and walked across the kitchen and into the living room. Lee was still sitting on the edge of the bed when Kay appeared in the bedroom doorway.

"I didn't expect to find you home, kiddo. Did you have a good trip?"

Lee nodded, forcing a bleary smile. Kay laughed at her expression, all too familiar with the symptoms herself. "So it was a late night, huh? Too much to drink? Give me a kiss and I'll leave you to your bed. Tellico is fine. I'll be back around three or so, and then I want to hear all about it."

Kay was still smiling as she bent down for a kiss. Lee tried to lose all her guilty feelings in her response, kissing Kay passionately.

"Umm, nice. I wish I could stay, but I'm off to town to see Mrs. Davis."

"Kay, I need to talk, really talk." Lee finally managed to force out some words.

"Sure honey. Can it wait 'til three?" Kay looked a little perplexed until Lee nodded.

"Okay, I'll see you then." Kay left after another quick kiss. Kay had been gone a long time when Lee staggered out to the kitchen. She put on the tea kettle and sat down at the table, trying not to jar her head.

Three o'clock seemed so far away, yet horribly near. How could she possibly explain last night? Maybe she didn't need to; maybe she could just let it go. Then mentally seeing Kay's trusting eyes once more, Lee knew that was impossible. Well it would just have to wait until later, when she could think clearly.

♌ ♌ ♌

By three-thirty, Lee was pacing in the kitchen. Lee was on the front porch when Kay finally drove up. Kay jumped out and came up to the porch. Lee caught her breath, seeing Kay's beauty in her every movement. Kay bounced up the porch steps two at a time, a wide grin animated her face.

"You're looking healthier," Kay laughed, gathering Lee in a bear hug. "I missed you. Did the interview go okay? Did you see your aunt?"

"It was a good trip," Lee answered vaguely. "Let's get a drink and sit in the kitchen. The flies are getting nasty out here."

Kay followed her back to the kitchen, humming a Heather Bishop tune to herself. Lee pulled out a pitcher of tea and poured two tall glasses full. She sat down opposite Kay, handing her one glass, and found herself smiling back at Kay's happy countenance.

"I really was surprised that I missed you so much last night. That's very unnerving to a self-declared hermit, you know." Kay's bright blue eyes danced. "So tell me all about it. Are you employed?"

"Not yet, but Greg Meeks made a great offer. I'll really have to think about it. He wants an answer in a couple of weeks."

"Did you visit your aunt?"

"Yeah, I saw her and Uncle Steve in the afternoon. I called Grandma too. It was fun. They said to say hello to you."

"So are you going to work for the paper?"

"I don't know, Kay. I'm really mixed up. The city was kind of fun, but I ended up wondering if it's the right place for me. I felt uneasy there. It seemed so dirty, and there were way too many people. I have a lot of thinking to do."

Kay nodded her understanding and then grinned again. "Now for the good part. What happened to put you in such a stupor this morning? Get picked up at the bar?"

"Yes, kind of," Lee admitted, and watched Kay's grin
fade as she saw the guilty expression in Lee's eyes.
"Is this what we need to talk about?" Kay's voice was
quiet now. Lee nodded.
"Well, so tell." Kay smiled, her darkening eyes not
joining in.
"It all began the other morning when I saw the hawk.
I felt as if I could see the world from her perspective.
It only lasted a few seconds and then I was me again,
but a little disoriented."
Kay nodded, waiting for more but not helping any.
Lee plunged on. "Then on Monday at the arts and
crafts festival it happened again. I was watching that
old fiddler play and got to wondering how it felt to be
him. And suddenly I was, but just for a few seconds. It
scared me. I should have said something then, 'cause I
know you picked up on it. But it seemed so weird, so
unreal. So I kept quiet."
"I wondered what was going on, but I figured you'd
get around to saying something when you needed to."
Kay's face was more relaxed as she waited for the rest
of Lee's story.
"When I drove into town I was thinking about it all,
wondering if it was ESP or what. I went to the interview, and it went well. Then a reporter for the paper,
Maggie Brown, took me out to lunch to answer questions and things. Well, she's a lesbian and knew I was
too, so we had a good time. Talking, you know? She
invited me to dinner and said we'd go to the bar." Lee
hesitated, trying to put everything together.
Kay waited, then spoke up impatiently. "How does
this tie in, Lee? What does Maggie Brown and the bar
have to do with the old fiddler?"
"I'm trying to explain, Kay. Just give me a second."
Lee felt nervous and irritated at the interruption. She
took a deep breath and started again.
"After lunch I felt kind of high just walking down
the street, enjoying the energy of the city. I was watch-

ing the people walk by wondering about them. So I decided to try to get into this young businessman's head. It didn't work at all. I was thinking this is stupid, when I bumped into this old woman. I apologized and noticed how sweet she looked. Next thing I knew I'm looking at myself through her eyes, feeling her body around me. Just for a few seconds and then I'm myself again."

"That's wild," Kay said momentarily forgetting any apprehension about Lee's visit to the bar. "Did it scare you this time? I'll bet you were beginning to believe it was real."

"Yeah, I was. And it didn't really scare me. I went to Aunt Grace's and sat around thinking about it all—the job and us, too. I drove back into town feeling bad about being there. In the city itself I mean. I met Maggie and we had dinner, drove around, and went to the bar. It was just like always—we drank and talked and danced. Lots of innuendoes, you know, but nothing serious. That is until we slow danced and I began to pick up on her a little bit. It felt good and I reacted like I used to. I pulled her close and enjoyed it."

Lee paused again aware that how she told the next part of the story was crucial. But she knew she wanted to be truthful, too. Kay was watching her face closely, as if looking for clues to what was so wrong.

"We danced and drank some more, and kept flirting a little. About one, Maggie took me to get my car. I was saying good night when I looked up and saw her eyes. That's when I wondered how she saw me and suddenly—poof—I knew."

"What happened?" Kay prompted when Lee hesitated again.

"Well, she was feeling pretty excited. You know?" Lee floundered.

"Horny?"

"Yes, and we were kind of drunk and . . . well, when I was back to myself I kissed her. That was a mistake

because I could feel the way she felt, too. Along with
my own reactions. It was . . . intense. So I kind of went
along with it, really got excited. Then something made
me ask myself what was happening and I stopped."

"Stopped?"

"Yeah, just tried to gracefully regroup. I scared myself and her too, I think. It felt pretty out of control."

"Honey, why are you so upset?" Kay's face was
smiling, half-incredulous. "You got drunk and a little
turned on. I admit this feeling her inner vibes is
strange, but I can't see why you're so upset. Nobody
got hurt, and I'm not either. It happens all the time."
Kay stopped when she saw Lee shaking her head
emphatically. She waited for more.

"That's just it. You don't understand. I knew how
she felt, everything she felt. I knew just what she
wanted, how to make her feel it all, in ways that I
shouldn't have known. It was as if I'd been her lover a
thousand times and knew her body like my own. Making love like that isn't for strangers, Kay, it's for lovers.
When two people make love like that, with that intensity and sharing, it's more than sex. To feel like all the
barriers are down. You're both wide open."

Kay was nodding, no longer feeling so safe. In a
quiet voice she said, "Yes, I know Leah. That's how we
would make love."

"Yes it is. But honey, Maggie felt it. Maggie knew
how close we came and so did I. I felt her; I knew her.
Now what do I say? How do I explain?"

Kay sat still, looking away from Lee, gradually com-
prehending the implications. Her face was carefully controlled, hidden, when she looked back at Lee. "All I
know to say is tell her the truth. Tell her how you feel."

Lee saw Kay's shuttered glance, and it hurt. She
knew her answer would too. "I don't know how I feel,
Kay. I know I love you, but I don't know who I am or
what I want. How can I commit to anything, make
plans with you, when I don't know myself well enough

to make plans at all? Part of me is a city girl and loves it. Part of me needs the country and can only exist there. I haven't decided which part of me I want to be, or if I can be both. So what do I say to Maggie?"

Lee stopped, tears of frustration in her eyes. Kay was staring at her, looking stunned. Lee felt as if she'd hit Kay, hurting her badly with her words.

"Shit. I wish I'd never started this," Lee whispered, looking down at the table.

The room was silent for a minute or two. Lee traced the wood grain of the old table, wondering what to say. She heard Kay sigh and glanced up to meet her eyes again. Kay's smile was a mockery, never reaching her eyes or changing the sadness in her gaze.

"It all needed to be said, Leah. I guess I was taking a lot for granted. We were getting ahead of ourselves. We haven't talked about a commitment to each other, or even made love yet. I don't even know how you feel about monogamy versus nonmonogamy." Kay tried to smile at her own attempt at levity. "You were right that first day at the falls. We can't rush this, if we want it to last. I think we have something special together, and you know that too. But I guess we have to slow down, give each other some space, get less intense maybe. At least I think that's the way to go."

"It sounds right, Kawi." Lee saw Kay wince at the use of her Cherokee name. Kay got up and started for the door. Lee grabbed her arm and held on until Kay stood quietly.

"I love you, Kay. I want us to work. Don't shut me out completely." Lee hugged Kay hard.

Kay hugged her too, kissing her hair, then stepped back to look into Lee's face. "I love you too, Leah. I'll be back tomorrow and we'll talk some more, maybe go for a ride. I'm not going to throw this away."

Kay bent and kissed her tenderly, then turned away. Lee stood watching her go, feeling very alone. As she shut the door, she fought off the need to call Kay back.

This is for the best, Lee said to herself; it has to be for the best.

That evening was too quiet for Lee as she sat reading. She tried putting music on, but all the lyrics kept conjuring up images of Kay. Lee put on a violin concerto and went back to her book.

She was startled when the phone rang. Half hoping it was Kay, she picked it up, ready to welcome her back. It was Aunt Grace instead. Her aunt talked for a while and then got to the point.

"I just talked to Mother. She'd like to come up next week and stay overnight, if that's okay. I thought I'd pick her up about four on Wednesday and be up there by five. We could eat down at the Sweet Shoppe and you two could have a good visit. I'd come back up on Thursday evening and take her back to our place for the night. Does that sound good, Lee?"

"That sounds wonderful, Aunt Grace. I'm planning to go back to town Friday, so maybe I could save you the trip. That is if Grandma wants to stay that long."

"Oh, I'm sure she'd be delighted. It practically took dynamite to get her down to Knoxville in the first place, you know. She'll want to stay, I'm sure."

They concluded the conversation with more general talk. Lee felt a thousand times better when she hung up. Grandma Brant was just the person she needed to talk to. Grandma could always cut to the bone of an issue, clearing away unnecessary waste. She'd help Lee settle herself, or at least be able to help clear Lee's mind on a few things.

Chapter 10

As the week continued, Lee spent several odd hours considering Greg Meeks's offer of a position on the Knoxville paper. She was all too aware that it was an incredible opportunity that she would have accepted immediately a year or more ago. Now she found herself looking for reasons to turn Greg down.

Maggie Brown also appeared often in Lee's thoughts. Lee felt a strange mixture of guilt, pleasure, and anticipation when she remembered Maggie's green-eyed intensity. Lee admitted that her interest in Maggie was reminiscent of several brief affairs she had waltzed through unthinkingly in Cleveland. Those romances had usually been fun and sweet, although she had not necessarily remained friends with her lovers afterward. This time Lee wanted to be friends with Maggie, to enjoy a close working friendship. She wondered if her undeniable sexual attraction to Maggie along with their interrupted embraces on Tuesday night had made a platonic friendship impossible. She fervently hoped not and tried to visualize conversations where they successfully made the transition from flirtation to friendship.

Kay was always foremost in Lee's thoughts. When she was alone, Lee often made note of her thoughts and observations to share with Kay. Kay's warmth and

gentle kindness seemed to encompass all of Lee's
memories of her friend. Lee knew that her love for her
old friend was continuing to grow in depth and inti-
macy. When Kay was absent, Lee felt a warm tenderness that swelled through her and caused her heart to
catch in an almost sweet, needy pain. When Kay was
near, Lee's body and mind seemed poised, waiting for
some momentous occurrence that could not long be
delayed.

Lee's desire and physical need for Kay also grew, despite their agreement to slow their developing relationship to a crawl. Lee knew her body would prefer a
galloping courtship that took them to bed immediately.
Out of respect for Kay's reserve and her own confusion, Lee kept her passion under firm restraint. But she
was aware that given even slight encouragement it
would run away with both of them. It grew harder and
harder for Lee to accept the rationale that kept control
of her desire for Kay, as Kay continuously responded
with warm, open tenderness when Lee was near.

Fortunately for their agreement to slow their sprout-
ing relationship Kay was inundated with work for the
last half of the week. She visited Lee daily but was
often on her way to an appointment or returning from
one. They had lunch together on Wednesday, but only
saw each other briefly on Thursday. It wasn't until a
shared, rushed lunch on Friday that Kay suggested a
trip together over the weekend.

"I talked to Mary and Fran last night," Kay began,
after finishing her sandwich. "Their friends from
Atlanta who I met last year are up this week for a visit.
They asked me to join them. I mentioned I was rather
preoccupied at the moment." Kay's smile was embarrassed, although her eyes rested warmly on Lee. "Mary
dragged the story out of me and invited you too. I
know it's short notice, but I think we'd have fun."

"I'd love to go, Kay," Lee answered with unqualified
enthusiasm.

"The only problem is we'll be stuck out back in one of the cabins. That was the only room left." Kay was watching Lee's response carefully, unsure of how this bit of information would affect her acceptance of the trip.

"Sounds nice and private," Lee agreed warmly, yet was unable to say more.

Kay smiled slightly, her blue eyes catching Lee off guard and constricting her heart. Then Kay seemed to withdraw once more into a careful protective reserve.

"There's a bed and a sleeper sofa in each cabin, so we can both be comfortable." Kay continued to explain as she finished her lunch. "I have appointments in Madisonville tonight, so I won't see you until tomorrow morning. Can you leave by nine?"

"I'll be ready," Lee promised and fell silent once more. Lee watched as Kay carefully stacked her dishes and carried them to the sink. She felt deep frustration with her own limitations and the decisions that had placed such distance between herself and Kay. Lee tried to conjure up some words or a phrase that would let both of them relax and reach out to each other once more. None came to mind.

"I'd better hit the road," Kay said and smiled sweetly at Lee, her eyes bestowing another tender gift.

Lee rose from her chair and walked to the door beside Kay, trying to understand what was happening between them. Kay's closeness and careful control added to her building frustration. Finally, as Kay turned to kiss Lee on the cheek, Lee acted out her desperation.

Lee intercepted Kay's lips with her own and then, through her kiss, made clear how her need for Kay had grown. Kay was unresponsive for a second or two; then her lips enveloped Lee's and her muscular arms gripped Lee's body.

Demanding passion supplanted Kay's usual tenderness, surprising Lee with its fire. As Kay's hands crept

under Lee's shirt and stroked her skin, Lee shivered uncontrollably. Lee felt Kay's grip tighten and Kay's
tongue slip between her lips, commanding a response.
Desire burst through Lee's last reserves, and her
body melted into Kay's. Kay moaned as her lips
pressed feverishly across Lee's neck. Lee felt heat flare
at Kay's every touch, but then she realized that Kay
was pulling away.

"No," Lee groaned plaintively, but she let Kay shift
back slightly. She felt Kay's body lose its warm supple-
ness and stiffen somewhat.

"I'm sorry. I shouldn't have gotten started," Kay murmured and kissed Lee's forehead quickly.

Lee gazed questioningly into Kay's eyes that were
now almost midnight blue with desire. Lee closed her
mouth just as she was about to ask Kay to stay.

"You have to go?" Lee asked.

"It's best, Leah," Kay breathed, wrapping her arms
about Lee once more. "We both need to think about
this and be sure. We'll have tomorrow night if we're
both certain."

"Promise you won't sit up talking to Mary and Fran
all night?" Lee tried to speak with levity.

"I promise," Kay vowed softly, and then broke her
hold on Lee. She stepped backward and grabbed the
doorknob, a tremor visible in her hand. "I have to go."

Lee nodded, not attempting to draw her back. Kay
stepped out the door and disappeared from sight. Lee
groaned audibly as Kay's Jeep started. She couldn't
imagine waiting another day before feeling Kay's touch
once more.

ᘒ ᘒ ᘒ

Lee's afternoon drifted slowly past. She attempted to
write but gave it up after several false starts produced
meanderings. After working purposefully in her garden
for more than an hour, she decided to ride. Tellico

welcomed her intentions and stood patiently while she brushed him and put on his tack.

Lee rode around the pasture once, checking the fences for damage and then turned for the road. She followed the dirt road down through the valley and then turned up the mountain ridge on a barely discernible path. It slanted up and backtracked in the direction she had come. This pathway degenerated quickly into a narrow deer track. Lee continued to urge Tellico onward up the hillside. Eventually they came to a small clearing, and Lee halted her horse to look down.

Below her, Grandma Brant's farm was spread out in miniature like a child's model. The red scar of the road ran past the farm and cut down the center of the small valley. Eventually it twisted upward through the trees to join Rafter Road, the main artery.

Lee straightened and looked across the valley to the opposite ridge. Slightly below her line of sight she could see the trees parting around Rafter Road. She watched a battered pickup's twisting ascent of the road. It became lost to sight in the deepening forest, but the noise of its engine bounced off the surrounding hillsides and reverberated through the quiet valley.

Lee's eyes searched higher and noticed several trees near the top of the ridge. The tips of the huge, old, loblolly pines could be picked out among the lighter-colored deciduous trees. Trying to visualize at what point on the opposite ridge the pine trees were located, Lee began to smile to herself. She realized those particular loblollies were part of the Pine Ridge Cemetery's leafy canopy. Slightly higher on the ridge was the Holt farm, but there was no break in the treetops to mark Kay's homestead. Lee smiled again and felt like a silly, romantic fool.

After she turned Tellico around and began descending the path, Lee let her mind picture Kay's lovely face. Her thoughts turned to their luncheon interlude and she shivered slightly, again feeling Kay's hands on her

skin. Lee shook her head, reminding herself to pay
attention to the narrow trail.

♌ ♌ ♌

Kay called about six-thirty.

"I had a terrible afternoon," she began and stifled a
laugh. "I was supposed to be consulting with Dr.
Rodgers about an upcoming fund drive. My mind kept
drifting back to lunchtime. Then he asked me if I was
ill. I sputtered out something about family problems
and tried to force my mind on business."

Lee joined her laughter, not admitting her own pre-
occupation of the afternoon.

"You'll be ready to leave at nine?" Kay asked. "I
thought we could stop at Bald River Falls on the way."

"That sounds wonderful. It's been more than ten
years since I saw it." Lee allowed her excited anticipation to steal into her voice. "I'll be ready by nine."

"Good." Kay's one syllable to reverberated with endless overtones in Lee's mind.

"Is someone going to take care of Tellico?" Kay
asked.

"He has more grass than he can eat, so he can keep
a day or two on just pasture. I asked Ralph Hartman to
check on him tomorrow evening. What arrangements
did you make about Dancy?"

"Doris McMurphy is sending over one of her boys to
grain her on Saturday and Sunday." Kay explained, her
voice suddenly restrained.

"Are you at Madisonville?" Lee asked, not wanting
Kay to end the conversation.

"Yes, at Margarette and Toni's. We ate already and I
wanted to call before I took off on my appointments."

"I'm glad you did, " Lee lowered her voice.

"Well, I guess I should go." Kay's intonation was hesitant and questioning. Lee realized that Kay wanted to
keep talking as well.

"I'd like to talk to you all night," Lee admitted as her voice dropped to an intimate tone. "But I guess that's silly."

"No, it makes perfect sense to me," Kay responded with humorous affection. "I've even thought about canceling everything or dropping in on you when I'm through."

"How about coming for breakfast?" Lee offered, although fervently wishing Kay would come immediately. Lee felt constrained by the continuing reserve between them and couldn't pursue what she dearly wanted.

"Okay," Kay said, "Is eight early enough?"

"Yes," Lee paused and then decided to end their halting communication. They both said good night. Lee heard the receiver click and replaced hers. She sighed deeply, still unsure why she hadn't told Kay to come to her after her appointments. Her thoughts were full of confusion and contradictions.

How could she be in love with someone, desire her, yet be afraid to make love? She thought about her experience with Maggie Brown and tried to imagine being faced with Kay's thoughts. Was that why she was afraid to go to bed with her?

It was that and much more, Lee silently admitted. It was childhood memories that held Kay so dear that Lee was petrified of hurting her. It was the thought of many of her own casual love affairs that seemed so promising and then dwindled away as unforeseen preconceptions warped them into impossibilities. Then there was this touch of madness, this gift of joining others' thoughts. Lee could not see what her future held when she contemplated this ability as a continuing part of her life.

"I'm afraid, Kay," Lee whispered softly, looking down at the telephone. "I'm so afraid of the future that I can't allow a present."

Tears of frustration and self-denigration welled in Lee's eyes. She fought back the black depression that sprang up immediately, trying to deny it a foothold in her thoughts.

"No, I'll read tonight. Then I'll be relaxed and ready for tomorrow," Lee promised herself, wiping away the tears.

She selected a favorite novel, *The Wanderground*, and began to read, forcing her mind to follow the printed images. Gradually her anxiety and frustration subsided, taking the blackness with them.

On Saturday morning, Lee rose early and walked to the barn. She fed Tellico some grain, cleaned and bedded his stall, and talked to him for a few minutes. She explained where she was going, how long she would be gone, and told him to expect Ralph Hartman. Tellico seemed to listen to every word, but Lee still felt foolish.

Lee took time to pour a huge amount of dry cat food in the bowl on the floor. A gray feline face with curious green eyes peered down from the hay loft, met Lee's glance, and then disappeared. Lee smiled to herself and left the barn.

She walked slowly to the house, enjoying the moist, cool, morning air. From the woods came the scent of flowering raspberry bushes. Lee breathed in deeply, reveling in the promise of sweet berries in the weeks to come.

Back in the kitchen, Lee began preparing French toast from a loaf of homemade bread that she had purchased from a nearby farm. Lee hummed tunelessly as she mixed up the batter and fried the first few pieces. She was pleased that Grandma Brant's old cast iron griddle heated so evenly and the bread fried in a beautiful yellow-brown flecked pattern.

Lee heard Kay's Jeep turn into the farm drive and met her on the front porch. Kay greeted her with an enthusiastic hug. Lee escorted her to the kitchen and served breakfast with a flourish.

Kay welcomed her portion with delight and wasted no time getting started. She interrupted her repast with a recounting of last evening's trip to Madisonville.

"I told you about Mrs. Parker, didn't I?"

"She has arthritis?" Lee was uncertain.

"Yes, but it seems to move from site to site in her body. I think it is actually an environmentally-induced reaction. I took her some more herbal tea and gave her a massage."

"Does the massage help?"

"It seems to provide immediate relief. I think the herbs are her best bet, since I haven't found the source of contamination."

"Did you get a chance to talk to Margarette and Toni?"

"Yes. They were quite perturbed with me for staying away. I finally admitted I was seeing someone new." Kay pushed a bite of toast around her plate.

"They want to meet me?" Lee asked, trying not to chuckle at Kay's delaying tactics.

"Yeah. I said we were busy this weekend, so Margarette suggested next Sunday. I can call it off if you'd rather not." Kay stabbed the long-suffering bit of bread and placed it in her mouth. She watched Lee speculatively as she ate.

"I want to meet your friends," Lee assured her. "As long as we're both free, it's fine."

"Good." Kay smiled and continued to eat with relish. "I didn't know you could cook."

"French toast is one of my few culinary accomplishments. Vegetable soup and tuna noodle casserole completes the list. I want to experiment some while I'm here and I have more time," Lee confided comfortably as she finished her breakfast.

"All done?" Kay asked, eager to be off.

At Lee's nod, she gathered the plates and silverware and rinsed them in the sink. Lee picked up her back-

pack and waited at the door. Kay joined her and held
the door open wide.

"After you, my dear," Kay bowed dramatically and
gestured to the open doorway.

Lee laughed, pleased with Kay's playfulness.

"How very chivalrous, Sir Kay," Lee intoned grandly
and strode through the entrance.

"Does that make you Arthur or Guenivere?" Kay wondered, following Lee down the front porch steps.

"I would prefer Morganna, I think," Lee answered
honestly.

"An evil sorceress?" Kay's eyebrows raised as she
slipped into the driver's seat of the Jeep.

"Don't believe everything you read," Lee warned with
a smile as the Jeep started.

"Did you read *The Mists of Avalon?*" Kay asked as
she turned the Jeep around.

"I relived it more than read it," Lee became suddenly
serious. "It was about six months before my accident.
I really felt it offered old perceptions I had studiously
ignored."

Kay drove up the dirt road in silence. Then she
turned onto Rafter Road and headed down the mountainside. Lee looked off through the trees, glimpsing
the panoramic view of the descending, forested mountain ridges and the bright blue sky.

"What about now?" Kay asked suddenly as she nego-
tiated a turn.

"What?" Lee asked, unsure of her reference.

"Do you still use those old perceptions?" Kay
glanced gaugingly at her and then turned back to the
twisting road.

"Yeah. In fact I've often wondered if my attempts to
become more open and intuitive reawoke my childhood abilities."

"That's possible," Kay nodded. "I know my own
healing abilities seemed to gather impetus, like a rock
rolling down a hill."

"Eventually it's a landslide." Lee shivered, suddenly chilled.

"Does that frighten you?" Kay gazed at her searchingly before being forced to look ahead once more.

"Yes," Lee admitted softly. "I'm afraid of it because I don't understand it. And I'm afraid of insanity."

Kay nodded once more. Her right hand gripped Lee's bare knee, and Lee covered it with her own. The warmth was comforting.

"I don't think I can stop it anyway." Lee sighed. "Let's forget for today, huh?"

"Sure." Kay readily agreed.

She pulled to a stop at the bottom of Rafter Road and took time to slip a tape in the cassette player. "Country Blessed" began to play and Lee joined in wholeheartedly.

Kay drove down the county route as quickly as possible, but its twist and turns made the trip slow. Lee relaxed and enjoyed the deepening wilderness that was drawing them ever farther into the mountains. On Kay's side of the road, Lee could see the Tellico River gushing over the rocks and slipping past tree-covered islets. On Lee's side, a towering wall of rock, covered with small trees and brush, rose perpendicularly, its deep, cool shadow chilling Lee's skin.

After the county route turned, the road to the falls gradually deteriorated. Kay slowed down and muttered to herself about the potholes she had to dodge. Lee continued to stare about her, overwhelmed by the grandeur of the deeply carved river valley.

At last they turned through a curve, came upon a two-lane bridge, and slowed to a stop. Lee sat speechless watching the water roar down on them, endlessly hurtling in white fury down the face of Bald River Falls.

"We can park on the other side." Kay had to speak loudly over noise of the steady torrent.

Lee nodded, remaining fixated on the waterfall as they drove across the river.

"Come on," Kay encouraged once they were parked in the nearly empty lot, and led Lee on foot to the middle of the span across the rapids.

Lee stood still, awed by the power of the water plunging over the rock face. The air was full of the smell of the river, a wet pungent musk that brought forth visions of the deep woods high above, where the river had been born. Lee drew a moist breath deeply into her lungs and felt her body join the deluge momentarily.

"It's wonderful," Lee said, realizing she was grinning foolishly. Kay laughed and grabbed her hand.

"Come on, we can climb above the falls."

Lee followed her up the steep, carefully constructed trail. They reached the top and stepped out on an overlying rock ledge that was surrounded by a guardrail.

Below them the water flowed, drawn ever faster to leap over the falls' lip and career downward to the rapids under the road bridge. Lee watched a green leaf join the water's descent. It was hurtled over the edge and lost completely in the pounding cataract.

"Follow me," Kay gestured, stepping past the guardrail. She led Lee down to a bare rock that jutted just above the falls' lip. Water droplets hit them sporadically as they gazed down the surging waterfall.

Lee looked down, feeling the pull of the drop. White water fell eternally downward, gathering power from the fall and emerging victorious as it buffeted the rounded boulders below. Lee blinked as dizzying vertigo seized her senses. She swayed forward, and then stepped suddenly back.

"It will draw you down," Kay spoke warningly into her ear over the deafening thunder of the falls. A strong arm encircled Lee and held her firmly on the bare rock ledge. Lee drew a deep breath and looked down once more. Now Bald River Falls was a spectacular natural phenomena of falling water and bristling rock. The spell had shifted. Lee smiled at Kay with a renewal of the excitement she had felt on the bridge. "It's wonderful! All the energy makes me feel high!" Kay nodded, grinning delightedly at Lee's reaction. They stood for several minutes gazing downward as they spray hit them occasionally, before Kay spoke again. "There's several small falls up river that people slide down."

"Will we go that way?"

Kay nodded. "We can. Are you ready to leave?" she asked.

"Yes," Lee shouted. Then she leaned close and kissed Kay's lips quickly. "Thank you."

Kay's arms tightened around Lee and she found Lee's lips once more, kissing her firmly. Lee pulled away, and Kay gazed sweetly into her eyes.

"I'm crazy in love with you!" Kay spoke loudly above the roar.

"I love you too," Lee answered without hesitation.

Kay's smile was as brilliant as the morning sun. "Let's go back to the Jeep," Kay urged.

Lee followed her, smiling to herself, already pleased with the day. They walked down the steep path side-by-side, bodies touching. A family of sightseers was coming up, so Lee stepped behind Kay to let them pass. Her unrestrained smile was answered enthusiastically by both parents and all four children.

When they reached the Jeep, Kay took the time to search for two county maps in the glove compartment. She peered at them and frowned.

"Looks like we can make it, but I better stop and ask." Kay smiled. "It'll be an adventure."

"I can imagine worse fates than getting lost on the mountainside with you," Lee commented as they proceeded upriver on the twisting road.

They passed a fifteen-foot falls where several swimmers were already at play. They were ignoring the signs that warned of the intrinsic danger in the falls'

undertow. In less than five miles, the road ended in a
large, heavily populated campground. Kay shook her
head in acknowledged confusion and went inside to
the camp office. She came back smiling with confidence.

"We have to backtrack about ten miles to the first
turnoff past the falls. After that we take all left forks.
The manager said it would get rough but we'd end up
just outside Marble. That's about ten miles from Mary
and Fran's."

"Let's try it," Lee urged.

♌ ♌ ♌

They passed the big falls and drove steadily for
several miles. Lee put another tape in the player and
listened to the music as they drove down the steep
river valley. They had crossed the river twice on narrow old iron road bridges when they saw the sign for
the turnoff.

Kay downshifted into second to climb the steep
ridge. The morning sun disappeared momentarily as
they passed through a narrow ravine. A fast-tumbling
creek rushed past them to join the larger river. Lee
breathed deeply and smiled as the cool, water-filled air
brushed past her face. Over the first ridge, a trackless
wilderness spread before them. Kay stopped the Jeep
and sat for a few minutes as they both silently sur-
veyed the rugged, forested landscape ahead of them.
Except for the narrow road, there was no sign of human habitation.

"We're in the Tellico Wildlife Area," Kay explained in
a voice hushed by the wilderness. She smiled and
asked, "Are you still game?"

"Just keep turning left," Lee confidently reminded
her. "We won't get lost."

"Okay." Kay put the Jeep in gear and they started
forward. The road wandered along the creekbed for ten

miles before the first fork took them up another hillside. As they drove continuously upward, Lee realized they were climbing the side of another mountain. Near the top, another fork took them on the less traveled dirt path. At the top of the ridge, another path slanted off to the right. Lee caught sight of a boarded up cabin.

"Old hunting cabin," Kay answered her unasked question before starting down the hillside.

A hundred yards down, a break in the trees provided an overlook. Kay put the parking brake on firmly and jumped out. Lee joined her as Kay stood silently gazing at the spectacular view.

Before them was the falling ridges of the mountain range covered by a dense canopy of leaves. The descending ridges formed knobby, gnarled fingers that reached out into the foothills below. Not until well into the foothills was there any visible evidence of humankind. In the blue haze of the distance, Lee thought she saw the land begin to flatten into the piedmont, but it was so far away that she knew it was probably her imagination.

"Welcome to North Carolina," Kay announced with a grin. "These are the Snowbird Mountains."

She pointed southeast past two ridges.

"You can just make out a break in the trees around Marble. That's where we're headed."

"It's almost a shame to go back down," Lee sighed.

"Yeah," Kay agreed, continuing to gaze across the foothills. "But it's lunchtime and I'm hungry."

Lee laughed and followed her back to the Jeep. Their descent was easy as the road became more and more traveled. Eventually the road ended on a state highway within a mile of Marble. In fifteen minutes, Kay parked the Jeep in a tree-lined parking lot in front of the Snowbird Highlands Inn.

Chapter 11

"Let's go find Mary and Fran," Kay urged, and started up a pathway paved in logs. Along the path a profusion of bright-colored flowers greeted their eyes.

Lee looked up at the lodge. It was a simple structure made of logs and stone, peeping out from a stand of deep green fir trees. Lee was just realizing the substantial size of the building when two women emerged from the screened-in porch that ran the width of the building.

The taller of the women swept Kay into a bear hug. Her deep brown eyes danced, and her tan face crinkled into a wide smile beneath her cropped gray curls.

"We'd just decided a cow had demanded your services, Kay."

"Oh Franny, we just took the scenic route," Kay grinned, hugging Fran firmly.

Mary had come to Lee's side and was welcoming her warmly.

"When Kay finally admitted you'd come back to the mountain, Lee, I couldn't wait to meet you. We've heard all about you two growing up together. Come on in. We've got a lunch buffet on the back verandah."

Lee looked into Mary's hazel eyes and felt instantly at home. Her light brown, straight hair was a third gray and cut into a simple bob. Her short, sumptuous body reminded Lee briefly of Dixie Holt until Mary smiled into her eyes again. Lee relaxed completely and fell in beside Mary, answering her friendly questions about life in Cleveland. The afternoon passed pleasantly. Lee met the lesbian couple from Atlanta as well as several other women who were staying in the lodge and some of the four outlying cabins. Fran told her their clientele was almost entirely women responding to the advertising in various lesbian periodicals.

Just before supper Kay and Lee retrieved their clothes from the Jeep and visited their cabin. It was a solid, square structure, sided with overlapping wood shingles. Inside they found a small bedroom, a bathroom with a tiny shower, and a large, open room that functioned as a kitchen, dining room, and den.

"This is wonderful!" Lee declared, looking over the clean, simple interior and pausing to inspect the glass door of the wood stove.

"It's great using the stove in the winter. The fire is so beautiful to watch," Kay reminisced. "I came over two years ago, and we hiked all day up in the mountains. There was an abandoned cabin along the old wagon road I would love to show you."

"Maybe tomorrow," Lee suggested as she turned to gaze at Kay.

Kay retreated slightly as if uncertain of Lee's intentions. Lee stepped across the intervening space, trapping Kay against the kitchen cabinets. She wrapped her arms around Kay and kissed her lips possessively.

"Let's come back here early, okay?" Lee murmured before Kay pulled her close.

Lee tried unsuccessfully to remain cool as Kay's lips invited her body closer. They melted together, the growing heat between them bonding them even tighter. After several minutes, Kay's lips found Lee's hair, and Lee's mind began to function once more.

"We're supposed to be helping with supper," Lee reminded Kay in a throaty whisper.

"Mmmmm," Kay's lips enveloped Lee's once more
and then pulled away to question her. "Think they'd
miss us if we just stayed here?"

"Fran would be insulted. She made taboulli just for
you," Lee said, letting her mouth pass over Kay's jawl-
ine to her neck.

Kay sighed deeply and placed her hands on Lee's
shoulders as if to push her away. Lee looked into her
deep blue eyes and seriously considered skipping
supper entirely.

"We can't, you know," Kay said finally, desire lower-
ing her voice to a husky murmur. "Mary would come
up here and pound on the door."

Lee laughed and stepped back, straightening her
shirt. Kay grabbed her hand and headed for the cabin
door.

♌ ♌ ♌

Supper consisted of taboulli, cheeses, fresh homemade bread, and an array of fresh fruit. On the side
board were sandwich fixings and cookies. Lee found
the cool, simple food delicious. She enjoyed talking
throughout dinner to Cindy and Pam who were from
Akron, Ohio.

After supper, the group gathered on the verandah.
Lee sipped with pleasure the wine-and-fruit mixture
Fran was serving, enjoying the pungent fruit blend. She
sat quietly, watching Kay animatedly telling a story
from their childhood years, about getting lost in the
mountains. She smiled to herself, remembering that
their panic had ended with Blackjack trotting into an
isolated farmyard where they were greeted by six other
children.

The evening drifted along, and Lee gradually felt the
wine take effect. She talked easily with several of the

women and enjoyed the balmy night air blowing through the porch screens. About ten she sought Kay out and touched her shoulder lightly.

"Are you ready?" she whispered and was surprised to see Kay reddened under her deep tan.

Kay nodded, her eyes skirting Lee's gaze, and started for the back door of the lodge. They were outside walking across the lawn when Fran intercepted them as she was returning from a storage shed.

"You two are leaving early," Fran's jovial voice filled the night air. "Tuckered out?"

Kay stopped, completely speechless before her friend. Lee could almost see her bright crimson blush through the darkness.

"I thought the cabin was too romantic to waste," Lee began quietly, her wide smile obvious in her voice.

"Be careful, Lee. Kay's broken hearts all over Tennessee and Carolina," Fran teased as Kay remained silent. "Just ask Mary's friend Becky. She's still hoping for another visit." Fran laughed easily. "Have a good night, you two."

"Oh lord," Kay murmured in a stricken voice as they walked to their cabin. "Now Mary will want a blow-by-blow description in the morning."

"Then I'll give her one," Lee answered comfortably, the wine's warmth still adding to her good humor.

"I'd be mortified," Kay declared as they stepped inside the cabin.

"You'll be too tired to care," Lee prophesized and wrinkled her nose at Kay's startled expression. "I'll shower first, okay?" At Kay's nod, she gathered her things and entered the bathroom.

Half an hour later, Lee awaited Kay in the bedroom. She sat up in bed sipping the last of the wine punch that she had carried up from the lodge. A small, single-bulb lamp burned on the other side of the bed. Lee was happy to sit in the shadows waiting for Kay to appear.

She felt tense yet excited, knowing the impending
lovemaking would finally allow the expression of her
needs and desire. But a part of Lee's mind was
strengthening the walls that had always separated her
from her lovers. Be careful, not too open; stay separate, it whispered. Don't lose yourself in the loving, or
love too much, it warned, because the inevitable pain
of parting will destroy you.

A silhouette was framed by the doorway; then
suddenly Kay was beside her.

"Hi," Kay said softly. Her half-smile was decidedly
nervous.

"I'm a little scared," Lee admitted, freed by Kay's
countenance. She looked down at her glass, swirled the
dregs of the punch then set it on the night stand.

Kay turned on her side and reached for Lee's hand.

"We can just hold one another," she suggested, her
voice calm and low.

"No." Lee's answer was immediate. She found Kay's
eyes and spoke slowly. "I want to make love to you,
Kay. I've never been in love like this. That's what
scares me. It's going to be very special."

"I know." Kay smiled. "Come here."

She drew Lee over and wrapped one arm around
Lee's shoulders. Their faces were close, and Lee smiled
as Kay's eyes twinkled in the reflected light. They lay
silent as Kay's hand softly caressed Lee's face.

"I used to imagine this night, years ago," Kay reminisced quietly. "I dreamed about holding you, kissing
you, and then making love. I finally had to put it away,
not let myself think of you. I told myself it would
never happen. But I kept searching for you in the
women I knew."

"Love me," Lee whispered.

Kay's arm tightened, pulling their bodies closer. Her
lips kissed Lee's forehead, eyebrows, eyelids, and nose.
Lee met Kay's gentle lips with her own, trying to express her loving feelings in that moment of tenderness.

Kay returned the kiss, letting her mouth linger as her hands began to caress Lee's body.

For a moment Lee pulled back and gazed into Kay's eyes. Kay's look was dark and deep, desire changing her eye color to the deepest sapphire. Kay reached for her again as Lee wondered what Kay felt.

Kay's warm lips drew Lee's with growing desire, as Lee felt a slight dislocation and saw a spinning spiral image in her mind's eye. Then she was encased in a strong, fluid body that held another woman close. Desire sang through her mind and soul. Her eyes opened, and she gazed on her beloved. Growing passion was tempered with a deep, tender regard that cherished every aspect of the woman she held.

Lee blinked and stared once more into Kay's gentle blue eyes. "You love me, really love me," Lee whispered.

Kay's mouth was Lee's only answer. It claimed her with a growing demand as Kay pulled Lee's body ever closer. Knowing the depth of Kay's love and desire, Lee was finally able to set fear and uncertainty aside and allow herself to respond to Kay's touch.

Kay's fingers lingered over Lee's back and then ran slowly down to caress her hips. Lee's hands drew Kay's face to her lips, and she flicked her tongue teasingly across Kay's mouth. Kay's tongue met Lee's through her parted lips, and as it stroked and explored Lee's mouth, Kay's fingers tightened spontaneously.

As their mouths separated, Lee gave voice to her uppermost thought. "I need to feel you against me, to touch you."

She pulled off her oversized T-shirt and helped Kay out of hers. Lee smiled, pleased to look on Kay's beauty in the dim light. Her fingertips started at Kay's neck and then flowed lightly downward between her breasts and across Kay's belly. Her fingertips came to rest in the dark hair between Kay's thighs. Lee let her fingers curl through the coarse hair and tug slightly before she bent forward to gather Kay's breast in her mouth.

The sweetness of this loving touch reverberated through Lee's thoughts, as her lips surrounded Kay's breast with kisses and her warm, wet mouth engulfed Kay's nipple. She licked and played gently on Kay's breast while her palm massaged the soft mound between Kay's thighs. Her fingertips caressed the folded skin hidden by Kay's legs. She heard Kay moan softly as her searching hand discovered a creamy wetness through which her fingers moved effortlessly. Lee continued to stroke playfully until Kay moaned again.

The sound pierced Lee's patience and she murmured to Kay in a throaty whisper. "I can't wait. I need to be inside you." Her fingers slipped easily between Kay's moist lower lips and found the pool of wet heat awaiting her.

"There," Lee whispered in satisfaction as her fingers slipped in, withdrew, then entered once more, and Kay's hips arched to meet her diving fingers.

"Oh yes!" Lee encouraged as Kay's body moved rhythmically. Then Kay's arms drew her down to passionate kisses that answered her thrusting hand. For several minutes, Lee's fingers glided deep into Kay's hot center, as she continued to kiss Kay deeply. Then Lee shifted, withdrawing completely from Kay's body.

"No," Kay groaned in desperate need, but Lee moved purposefully. She kneeled at the lower end of the bed and spread Kay's thighs with her hands. As her mouth touched Kay's wet, nether lips Kay gasped. Lee's tongue slipped through the moisture to dip into Kay's core. Lee submerged her tongue in the wet pool and then let it run upward to find Kay's swollen clit. Kay gasped again. Then she began to moan as Lee's tongue started a slow steady stroking from deep in Kay's center upward to her clit once more.

Lee listened to Kay's breathing, gauging her growing need, and then drew back again. Before Kay could protest aloud, Lee's fingers entered her hot core and pushed deep. Lee's tongue remained on Kay's clit and began a slow rhythm. Lee felt Kay's hands grip her hair, pressing her face against Kay's body. Lee's joy gave her added pleasure in her erotic task as she used her mouth and hands to bring Kay growing ecstasy.

Lee pushed her fingers deeper, constantly deeper, as Kay's hips thrust forward and apart, encouraging this exploration. Kay demanded a quickening rhythm and Lee responded, feeling Kay's internal muscles tighten with every stroke.

"Yes, oh yes," Lee murmured aloud her excitement, then returned to her loving as Kay moaned. Lee answered Kay's need with greater intensity; then she heard Kay cry out. Her fingers were squeezed as muscles contracted deep within Kay's body. Lee moved slightly with the rhythm, adding to the cascading ecstasy that filled Kay's being.

Afterward Lee joined Kay, stretching out on the bed with a satisfied sigh. Kay opened her eyes and attempted a smile.

"Hello," Lee whispered, and kissed her cheek. Kay's smile widened.

"You're wonderful," Kay sighed and caressed Lee's cheek with a tentative hand.

Lee smiled, meeting Kay's gaze with a steady tender look. Kay suddenly laughed and pulled Lee on top of her. "And I was all prepared to gently seduce you," she chuckled and kissed Lee's wet lips firmly. "Instead I just lay there and moaned."

"I enjoyed the sound effects," Lee teased. "In fact I enjoyed your every response. I hope you did too."

Kay laughed again and drew Lee's lips to hers once more, as the musky scent of love encircled them. This time their kiss deepened, and Lee felt her body begin to ache in anticipation. Kay's arms tightened, and she rolled over, pinning Lee beneath her.

"There," Kay's voice was satisfied. "Now I can finish what I started." She smiled at Lee's solemn face and kissed her nose before becoming more amorous. Lee closed her eyes, as Kay's mouth and fingers began to play across her body.

At first, Kay's lovemaking was a teasing promise, searching out Lee's hidden spots that suddenly responded intensely. A lick on her inner elbow, a soft bite to her inner knee made Lee tense with excitement. Then Kay's lips returned to Lee's breasts and began a thorough entreaty, asking for every response of which Lee was capable. By the time Kay's mouth traveled slowly down between her thighs, Lee felt only a gripping need.

Kay moaned as her tongue slipped into Lee's dripping lower lips. Lee shuddered as Kay's tongue teased over her, tickling her clit and flitting over her center. Kay continued to play until Lee arched to meet her, trying to catch her elusive tongue. Kay murmured softly and placed her hands on Lee's legs, spreading her wide. Lee cried out as Kay's tongue dove deeply into her and moved constantly, making her burn.

Then Kay's mouth moved upward. As Kay sucked Lee's hardened clit between her soft lips, her fingers pushed slowly into Lee's core. Lee cried out as Kay's fingers stroked her internally, and Kay, still holding Lee's clit in her lips, moved her tongue across it.

Lee tried to relax, hoping to prolong this incredible joy, but Kay was relentless as her fingers moved and her tongue excitedly demanded a response. Lee felt her body stiffen and heard a low groan tear from her throat. Her deep, inner muscles contracted, sending waves of ecstasy through her body. Kay lay quietly between Lee's legs, her head resting on Lee's thigh as the contractions diminished.

Lee breathed deeply, with her eyes still closed as her body regained a sense of balance. Then a flame began to lick across her skin and play around her clit, flicking across it only after Lee's hands curled in Kay's hair. Kay's tongue continued to dance seductively from Lee's clit, about her lips, and across her heat. Lee's only thought was to follow the lead of Kay's tongue. After several intricate contortions, it dipped into her aching wetness. Her soft gasp brought it back, accompanied by a questing finger. As Kay's light touch repeatedly drew a dripping response, Lee's hips acknowledged the seduction was complete.

Lee gasped as Kay's finger moved into her, and she thrust herself upward to force Kay's touch into her depths. Kay's hand and tongue moved slowly, and Lee realized Kay's intention to prolong the loving. Lee relaxed and sighed with gratification as Kay added another finger to her probing thrusts. Lee spread herself wide and heard Kay groan as her fingers plunged deeper into the fluid heat.

"Oh, woman!" Kay murmured in husky praise, and her rhythm slowed even more.

Lee lay still and let her thoughts drift outward. She touched Kay's mind and joined it easily. She felt momentary guilt as there was no knowledge of her presence, but that was soon lost as Lee thrilled to Kay's thoughts and feelings.

She knew Kay's resolve to love her all night and smiled knowingly as Kay's fingers descended with ecstatic slowness into her once more.

Timelessness became the rhythm of their lovemaking. Lee knew both their bodies and slowed her own response as she anticipated Kay's impending touch. They both stopped thinking of anything but the warm wetness under Kay's fingers and the throbbing clit under her tongue.

Lee was not sure when awareness of a growing intensity began, but both she and Kay felt it rising. They continued their slow lovemaking as Lee's body grew hotter under Kay's touch. Lee couldn't remember ever feeling such exquisite, fevered desire as the fire burned deliciously within her.

Kay thrust downward, moaning softly, and Lee knew her ardent excitement. Lee tightened slightly, as Kay pushed further, and felt the heat flare within both of them. It suddenly flashed up and out, consuming her. Lee cried out and gripped Kay's shoulders with painful strength. Convulsions tore through Lee, and her body shuddered with prolonged pleasure. Lee lost track of place and self as her body soared with ecstasy.

When Lee returned, Kay was beside her watching her carefully. Lee tried to smile and breathed deeply. Kay's eyes softened and she settled beside Lee with a sigh. Lee's head found her shoulder and they lay silently, their bodies relaxing.

"Sleepy?" Kay asked.

"No," Lee murmured. "Just resting up."

"Good." Kay smiled and her hand slipped possessively over Lee's breast.

Lee allowed her body to rest while her mind drifted through erotic imagery. Eventually she turned slightly and let her fingers caress Kay's thigh. Kay moaned softly and spread her legs to allow Lee's touch to slip inward. Lee murmured Kay's name as her fingers slipped into a waiting warm, wet creaminess.

A rhythm began in both women's response, and lovemaking took hold of their bodies once again. They both knew that this night was to be an endless joy, and their bodies claimed it effortlessly. Through the night, desire continued until sleep caught them in the act of love and stilled the rhythm for a few hours.

♌ ♌ ♌

Kay's travel alarm rang at a quarter past eight. Lee groaned as she tried to open eyelids weighted shut. Kay flopped on her stomach, one arm over Lee's body, and it remained there, a dead weight.

"Why am I awake?" Lee demanded of the world at large.

Kay's head moved slightly so her words were discernible despite the pillow.

"Breakfast's at eight-thirty."

"Oh, breakfast."

Lee tried to imagine eating soon but was distracted by Kay's nearness. She turned on her side, ignoring the heavy presence of Kay's arm and peered at the woman beside her.

"Will someone come and get us if we don't get up?"

"Fran might . . ." The rest of Kay's answer was lost in her pillow.

"What did you say?"

Kay sighed deeply and turned on her back. "I said Fran might turn up any time, especially after your glibness last night."

"Well, we couldn't have just ignored her." Lee smiled, undisturbed by Kay's complaint.

She lifted her hand and ruffled Kay's unruly hair. As Kay turned to smile at her, Lee was surprised to feel her desire stir by such a limited touch. She let her hand slip downward to settle on Kay's breast.

"I think we should wait a while for breakfast," Lee suggested, watching Kay's eyes darken as her fingers stroked softly.

"Yes, you're right," Kay whispered.

It was nine-thirty before Kay led the way up the back steps of the lodge. They found sweet rolls still sitting on the sideboard in the dining room. They had sat down next to each other when Fran entered from the kitchen. She smiled sweetly at Kay, who glowered in response.

"I don't want to hear it," Kay warned.

"What?" Fran asked in all innocence. "I was just going to say good morning."

Kay continued to eat silently, refusing to give Fran any additional ammunition. Lee watched the interplay with hidden delight.

"How did you ever get Kay to sleep so late, Lee? She's usually such a morning person, so bright and chipper."

Fran's eyes danced while Lee tried to swallow a bite of her sweet roll as she laughed. Kay broke the silence. "Don't encourage her." Kay glared at Lee, her eyes suspiciously bright. "She'll go on all day if you let her get started."

Lee was searching for the proper retort when she was saved by Mary's bouncing entrance.

"So you two sleepyheads decided to eat. Do you have plans for the day, or are you just going back to bed?" Mary's face was controlled, devoid of the slightest hint of a smile.

"Oh lord," Kay snorted in disgust, but she broke into a grin as her eyes met Lee's.

"Actually we haven't made any plans," Lee began after her laughter quieted. "Kay was telling me about an abandoned cabin she hiked to a couple winters ago."

"That's a long walk," Kay protested.

"Not if you go up the fire trail," Fran explained. "I remember we took the old wagon road that day, so it was more than twice as far. It's only a couple of miles up the fire road."

"I'd love to see it," Lee admitted and Kay smiled at her.

"Why not?" Kay agreed softly, her look tender. She glanced up to see Fran's smiling wink at Mary. "What are you two grinning at?" Kay bristled.

"I've never seen you so sweet and docile, Kay. It's quite charming," Fran began.

"Yes, you're usually grousing about work or muttering about some plant you have to look for up on the mountain by now," Mary commented as Kay blushed.

"You seem to have a civilizing effect." Fran cocked her head at Lee. "To what do you attribute your success?"

"Exhaustion," Lee answered solemnly.

Fran nodded sagely, as if expecting this answer, then turned back to Kay. As Fran was about to speak, Kay jumped up and headed for the back door.

"I don't need to hear this," she shouted over her shoulder, laughter evident in her tones.

Lee shrugged at this response, meeting Fran's inquisitive look with a smile.

"Come into the kitchen, Lee. We'll make a lunch for you to take." Mary smiled warmly.

Lee followed her into the huge kitchen and began to assemble sandwiches as Mary produced the fixings. Mary continued to work as she asked Lee about her stay on the mountain and her future plans. Lee found herself talking easily, relating her concerns and uncertainties about the months to come.

"Things usually work out if you're willing to keep trying," Mary observed. She caught Lee's eye and her face crinkled into a gentle smile. "Fran and I weren't completely joking, you know. I've never seen Kay so happy."

"We've been friends for a long time," Lee equivocated, uncertain of what else to say.

"Every once in a while Kay would tell a story about you two, like she did last night. It used to worry me. I used to think she'd keep looking for someone like you, someone that was really more dream than memory." Mary stopped and seemed to search for words.

"And now I'm back," Lee prompted.

"Now you're back, and I'm hoping you two have more together than just the past." Mary's face was composed, but her eyes searched Lee's worriedly.

"I think we do, Mary. I really do," Lee assured her, suddenly certain herself.

"I'm glad." Mary smiled, though her eyes still gauged Lee's response.

"Me too." Lee answered, meeting Mary's glance with a happy smile.

"Here. You two go hike in the highlands." Mary handed the completed sack lunch to Lee. "I'll keep Fran occupied until you get away."

♌ ♌ ♌

Lee was still smiling when she walked into the cabin. Kay was seated at the tiny kitchen table writing in a notebook. She looked up as Lee entered. Her countenance turned Lee's smile to laughter.

"You'd better not look at me like that in front of Fran," Lee warned.

"Oh, Franny will get used to it." Kay rose and walked to the door. "She and Mary have been the doting couple for years. Are you ready for a hike?"

"Lunch and all." Lee kissed Kay on the nose. "Shall we go?"

They started out the cabin door and angled across the huge yard. Kay led Lee to a wide path that disappeared into the woods behind the cabins.

"This crosses the fire trail in about one hundred yards," she explained as they began their ascent.

The fire road was one vehicle wide and headed due northwest. As they climbed the first rise, Lee was surprised to feel the pull in both of her legs. Looking ahead in dismay, she saw the road made little accommodation for the steep grade.

"We'll take it slow," Kay assured her, as if she felt Lee's uncertainty. "That's why we used the old wagon road last time. Our ancestors were much more sensible road builders, at least from the walker's viewpoint."

Lee was glad to relax and walk slowly. It gave them a chance to talk and look about the woods that surrounded them. Kay began to identify some of the plants along the trail. This brought back memories of Grandma Dixie and their excursions together on the mountainsides in search of various herbs. Lee loved to hear Kay speak of Dixie Holt and cherished the insights that Kay's stories provided.

They had climbed steadily for more than an hour before Kay began to recognize landmarks. Within a few minutes after that, they came to the intersection of the settler's old wagon road and the modern fire trail. Kay stopped for a moment and turned to Lee.

"It's just a short way from here to the cabin, I think. Do you want to take a breather?"

"No, let's keep going." Lee was happy the climb was nearly ended. "We can sit and relax once we get there."

Kay nodded her agreement and started up the wagon road. It angled sideways across the mountain with much less incline than the newer fire road, out of deference to the people and livestock that had climbed it a century and a half before. Lee felt her body's positive acceptance of the less arduous trail.

They had hiked only a few hundred yards when they stepped into a partial clearing. Ahead on a level area stood the bare bones of an ancient cabin and barn. Just the age-blackened logs remained in position. The roof and doors had disappeared under the assault of time.

The two women walked quietly to the small cabin and stood awkwardly near the door. Both were hesitant to go farther.

"Look." Kay's voice was hushed. "Sage and rosemary." Kay bent down and plucked a gray-green leaf from the sage bush that was growing beside the doorway. She rolled the leaf in her fingers and brought the fragrant herb to her nose, inhaling deeply.

Lee tried to see in the cabin, then stepped to the entrance to peer into the shadowy interior. The single room was all of twelve feet by sixteen. Nothing remained inside but the logs themselves, some sparse grass, and a scraggly bush.

Lee pulled back, not wanting to enter. Unthinkingly she laid her hand on the door jam. "I wonder who lived here?" Lee asked softly, expecting no answer.

Four faces flashed into her vision, and she stepped back, startled by the abruptness and clarity of the images. She felt Kay's arm encircle her, and Kay propelled her away from the ruined cabin walls.

"I'm sorry," Lee began.

"It's all right. Let's walk over to that rock and sit down," Kay suggested. Her voice was constricted, and she continued to hold Lee tightly.

Lee nodded, and they walked back to the edge of the clearing. They settled on a huge slab of rock that protruded from the ground. The bright sunshine and the warmth of the rock dispelled Lee's initial dismay.

"I saw them," Lee began to explain. She paused as Kay nodded.

"I know. I did too." Kay whispered tremulously.

"What?" Lee was amazed. "What did you see?"

"Four faces. The two children were the sharpest." Kay's face was intent as she related her vision. "A young girl, about fifteen, was the clearest. She had long, straight, blonde hair and a narrow, elongated bony face. The boy was towheaded, almost white-haired. He was eleven or so. His face hadn't lengthened yet, but he was obviously her brother. They both had blue eyes, looked a little dirty, and were dressed in dark blue clothes. They were both very solemn. The parents had darker hair, almost black. The man had a full beard, but it was neatly trimmed. They both were farther away, in the background almost. They were dressed in black."

Lee had become very quiet, looking down at the ground as Kay spoke. At the end of the description, she questioned Kay.

"Did you feel anything when you saw them?"

"Yes." Kay's voice was assured although hushed. "A deep, keening sadness. My chest tightened up, and I felt ready to cry."

Lee looked into Kay's face again, her eyes uncertain, almost baffled. "You saw exactly what I saw. You had the same emotional response. How can that be?"

Kay shook her head. Obviously, the experience had shaken her composure badly. "I don't understand it. It's never happened before." Kay closed her eyes briefly as if to dispel the memory. "It hurt."

"Their pain was very real," Lee agreed, still baffled.

"Let's walk back to the fire road," Kay said suddenly, standing up and beginning to walk away. "I need to get away from here, I need to move."

Lee jumped up and followed with her friend. They walked silently back to the fire road. Lee thought about their joint experience and began to piece together a theory about its origin. She felt great relief to step into the open, sunny, roadway when they reached it. It felt good to see it stretching invitingly in both directions.

"Come over here and take a break," Lee ordered as she plopped down on a grassy knoll. She began pulling sandwiches and apples from the sack lunch she carried. Kay remained silent as they ate, apparently preoccupied. As they finished some cookies, Lee tried to get Kay to talk.

"Are you all right about this?" Lee asked, worried by Kay's continued silence.

"I think so." Kay's voice was uncertain. "I can understand now why it's so hard for you. It comes so unexpectedly, so totally, and overwhelms your mind. How did you ever make peace with it?"

"I haven't yet," Lee admitted softly, and grabbed Kay's hand.

"It comes to you like this too? Without choice?"

"Sometimes it's a sudden, complete picture. This time I asked though," Lee reminded her.

"Why did I see it?" Kay's wide blue eyes looked into Lee's, demanding an answer.

Lee turned her eyes away and looked down the fire road. She wished desperately that she could keep her theory from Kay, but she knew that would be unfair.

"It's because of last night," Lee said firmly, trying to hide the fear that this admission brought to her.

"Last night?" Kay repeated, dazed with confusion.

"When we made love," Lee paused, and then forced the words out. "I reached out to you, was with you twice. I think that link isn't totally broken."

"With me, in my mind?" Kay's emotions stormed across her face, leaving Lee silent and guilty.

"You didn't say anything. You didn't even ask." Kay whispered and turned away. She shook off Lee's hand as Lee tried to physically communicate her apology.

"Was that why?. . . Did you know how? . . . " Kay halted momentarily. Then her words became precise. "Did you use it to manipulate me?"

"No." Lee pulled Kay around and looked into her agonized eyes. "No. I joined you the first time before we started. I understood then that you love me, really love me."

Kay nodded, her eyes locked on Lee's, pleading silently for a reprieve from this invasion.

"Then I joined you again when you made love to me. The second time, when it was slow."

Lee felt tears on her cheeks as Kay continued to stare stiffly at her, completely appalled by Lee's perfidy.

"I wanted to join you, feel your desire, your joy. It was wonderful to reach out for you physically, yet be part of your response." Lee hesitated, seeing the doubt in Kay's eyes. She raised her hand and caressed Kay's cheek. "I would never use that ability, that knowledge, to ensnare you. I couldn't. I love you."

Lee waited, watching Kay's face for a clue. Kay still gazed into her eyes for several moments, as if divining the truth, and then looked away. For a few minutes,

Kay was silent. She picked up a blade of grass and began to shred it into small pieces. Lee waited, knowing no words from her could hurry this process of emotion and thought.

Finally Kay sighed deeply and turned back to Lee. "I'm really hurt and angry that you could invade my privacy so easily without seeming to understand why it was wrong." Kay waited for Lee's silent nod of acknowledgment before continuing. "I'm also frightened and disturbed that your abilities seem to link us without my knowledge or consent."

Again Lee nodded, although frightened by Kay's withdrawn, controlled tone.

"I need time to think about this. Time alone." Kay's face finally broke into a grimace of despair. "I love you so. Last night was wonderful. But I can't stand the thought of not knowing you're inside my mind, when you are. I'd have to know. I'd have to have some control."

Lee gathered Kay into her arms and held her. She pressed her cheek into Kay's soft hair and held on firmly as Kay sobbed silently.

"I promise," Lee whispered. "I promise I'll never use it again with you. Never. It's too much power between us."

♌ ♌ ♌

The rest of the afternoon passed in an uncomfortable blur of sadness and tension. The walk to the lodge was interminable. They said their good-byes quickly, leaving Fran and Mary confused and questioning about their changed behavior. The drive back to Grandma Brant's farm on the main highways was long and virtually silent.

It was not until Kay parked the Jeep and followed Lee into the house that Lee felt a glimmer of hope. Kay was hesitant about leaving. Then she began to ask meaningless questions and offer tidbits of thought about the day. Lee finally realized that Kay didn't want to leave without some resolution of their disagreement.

Lee walked over as Kay stood by the door and kissed her firmly. She encircled Kay in her arms, holding her lightly, hoping for a response. Kay's answer was melting warmth and a tight embrace.

Lee broke off their kiss and spoke softly, not allowing any interruption. "I'm sorry I was a stupid fool last night. I'm sorry if I hurt you. I love you. I was wrong last night, but what happened wasn't. We made wonderful, glorious love, and I want that again, too. Now go home and think about it."

"Okay," Kay agreed, before kissing Lee deeply once more. Then she was gone, quickly and quietly, leaving Lee uncertain of Kay's true feelings. She sighed and admitted to herself that only time would answer her questions.

Chapter 12

For two days Lee suffered through a self-proscribed abstention of all contact with Kay. She spent her time writing, gardening, and riding Tellico. In the evenings she listened to music and read whatever kept her interest.

Lee didn't phone Kay or allow herself to even consider a visit to the Holt farm. Lee knew she must give Kay all the time she needed to reconsider their relationship in light of her own selfish misuse of her abilities.

It was past eleven on Tuesday evening when the telephone awoke Lee from the light sleep of first slumber. She stumbled to the living room and found the receiver in a sleepy haze, wondering vaguely if it was an emergency call.

"Hello?" Lee demanded, trying to sound awake.

"Hi, Lee. It's Kay."

Kay's voice sounded odd. Lee's mind jumped to fearful conclusions as she came fully awake.

"Are you okay?"

"Yeah. I just need to talk. I woke you up, didn't I?"

"Yes, but that's okay. I've been hoping you'd call."

"I needed the time, but I missed you."

"I missed you too."

Lee wanted to continue, wanted to demand what Kay
had decided, but forced herself to silence. Her fingers
tightened on the phone as Kay remained silent. Finally,
after a long minute, Kay's voice came over the line.
  "I guess I don't know how to say this."
  "Go on, " Lee encouraged, resolving to remain brave.
  "I want—I need to see you again." Kay's voice continued soft and low. "I realize I love you, not just who I
thought you were. Not just my memories. I think we
can work it out, if you really meant what you promised
on Sunday. If you really won't try to use your ability
with me again."
  "I promise," Lee reiterated, hoping her voice sounded
truthful and sincere.
  "Okay," Kay paused, evidently uncertain. "Maybe we
can get together later in the week. I'll call or something."
  "I'll let you know if I come up with something to
do," Lee said, pushing away thoughts of Kay coming to
her bed tonight.
  "I'll be in touch," Kay promised.
  "Good night," Lee answered, then hung up.
  Lee sighed and purposefully kept away thoughts of
self-recrimination. What had happened was over. Now
she must begin again and rebuild Kay's trust in her.
She walked back to the bedroom and lay down, surprised at her sudden tiredness. Lee smiled sleepily as
she remembered Kay's soft admission of love. She imagined Kay's arms aroud her and drifted into sleep.
  The next morning, right after she got up, Lee called
Kay, catching her before she headed out on calls. She
reminded Kay of Grandma Brant's impending visit and
apologized profusely for not remembering to speak of
it the previous night. Then Lee invited Kay to eat with
her family at five. "Maybe you could come early,
around four?"
  "Sure. Do you need me to bring anything?" Kay's
voice was tentative and slightly tense.

"Just some help with the cooking."

"Damn, I was hoping this was an indecent proposition," Kay joked weakly, attempting to relieve the tension between them.

"It is, woman," Lee laughed. "That's why I want at least one hour alone with you."

"I'll be there with bells on!" Kay promised with a warm chuckle, her tone relieved and near normal.

Lee felt wonderful as she walked out to feed Tellico. It had seemed like the whole world had crumbled Sunday. But it was going to be rebuilt again, even if she had to do it stone by stone, Lee promised herself.

She fed Tellico and brushed him while he ate. She apologized for not riding much lately and promised a short ride the next day.

When Lee walked out of the barn, she noticed a board had been pulled off the corner of the barn and was laying nails up in the pasture. She got a hammer and nails, and went through the gate to pick up the board. Lee nailed it back into place and wondered why Tellico had bothered to tear it off. Boredom, or did he need minerals to balance his diet? Lee asked herself. As she was finishing, Tellico walked out of his stall and came over to see what she was doing.

"You should leave the barn alone, Tellico. It's an antique, you know. I'll get you some additives at the feed store, if you need something beside that sweet feed." Tellico looked at her, not answering. His big brown eyes looked solemn, but friendly. Lee looked at him, wondering how horses saw the world.

She was looking at herself. There was no warning dizziness this time, no transition at all. She stared at the woman who looked vacantly back and then walked away. Walking with four legs was a strange sensation, but Lee realized that Tellico was a marvelous athlete with just those four steps. His muscles were firm, strong, and finely adjusted for any need. He was aware of almost every movement around him, and prepared

to react instantaneously. Yet Tellico was an integral
part of the natural world. Lee could feel few barriers
between his concept of his self and the rest of the
physical world. His body and mind reflected the infinite changes in the world around him, and it reflected
his. Tellico stretched down his neck to pluck a particular stalk of grass. It was just the right taste to go with
the grain already in his stomach. His lips and tongue
searched it out and tore it off, without the aid of his
eyes.

Lee found herself back in her own body again with
little transition. She watched Tellico walk away, feeling
awed by his abilities. It was like visiting the body of an
Olympic athlete, she thought. She knew he was totally
focused, totally sure of his capabilities, yet gentle and
kind. Lee shook her head in amazement. No wonder so
many people lost their hearts to these animals.

Lee walked back to the house thinking about other
animals on the mountain rather than her breakfast.
She could learn so much, share such wonderful insights if it was possible for her to continue to use this
new ability. It reminded Lee of stories she had read
about Native Americans joining other beings during
fasts and ceremonies. She had read claims in books on
spirituality that it was an ability all humans had had at
one time but had lost over the centuries. Could she
learn to use it for longer periods, direct it better? Why
didn't it work with all people? How could she use it
wisely, ethically, so not to offend the integrity of the beings around her?

Lee's steps slowed as she wondered about her own
response to this strange, intrusive ability. Kay had been
so outraged, so overwhelmed by the presence of uncon-
trollable images in her mind. Why had she not felt the
same?

Lee pondered the question, trying to ignore the mixture of guilt and shame she felt, remembering instead
Kay's reaction and her own thoughtless intrusion into

other's minds. Perhaps her lack of shock, never even
questioning her own ethics, was because of the presence of this ability from her earliest years. Her own
mind had never been totally controlled, never completely her own at any time in her life. Maybe this life-
time of experience had left her blinded to the serious
affront others would feel if their mental integrity was
breached. Lee smiled ruefully to herself as she admitted this last conclusion sounded suspiciously like self-
serving rationalization.

Lee shrugged slightly, acknowledging her own inabil-
ity to completely understand herself or others. She
made a silent, solemn vow to use her ability as morally
and ethically as possible. Lee knew she would have to
ask Kay's help to understand the ramifications this ability had for others. Kay would help her learn to direct
and control it, as well.

During the day, Lee drove to town to buy supplies
for dinner. She wanted to serve Grandma Brant in her
own kitchen, not at some restaurant. During the drive
to and from town, she continued to wonder about her
new gift, how it could be used, and whether it could be
strengthened.

After returning to the farm, she also thought hard
about Kay and their relationship. Lee became determined to reassure Kay that she really loved her. She
didn't want to lose their closeness by any misuse of
her abilities. She daydreamed about the future, trying
on several possibilities. The dreams all ended with the
two of them making passionate love to each other.

Maggie Brown's face swirled up several times, unbid-
den. Lee felt guilty, felt she should call Maggie and see
her on Friday. She was aware of just how easy it would
be to become sexually involved with Maggie. Lee knew
they would have fun together, enjoying the city and
each other. She also realized that she would be turning
back the clock to the Lee who had existed before the
accident. In many ways that felt impossible, Lee

thought, but was living in the mountains a viable alternative?

♌ ♌ ♌

A little after four Kay appeared at the back door. She was carrying a big Florida watermelon and some summer squash, her contribution to dinner. Lee barely gave her time to put it all down before she gave her a big hello kiss.

"That feels good," Kay said, somewhat tentatively. Lee smiled, then tried again. This time Kay held her close, returning the kiss with enthusiasm.

"God, that makes me wish Grandma was coming to-morrow," Lee said with a sigh. "I've been missing you all day."

Kay laughed, looking down at Lee as if Sunday's anger were completely forgotten. The expression in her blue eyes made Lee forget everything but the two of them, as Kay pulled her into another passionate embrace. They were kissing deeply when they heard the sound of a car turning onto the dirt road from Rafter Road.

"Oh no, that can't be them," Lee prayed aloud.

But she knew it was her aunt's car before the big cream-colored sedan came into view. Giving Kay one more quick kiss, Lee turned to check the roasting chicken.

"I can't believe they're this early. The food is no-where near done, and I wanted some time with you." Lee stood looking out the window.

"It's okay, honey," Kay whispered in Lee's ear, wrapping her arms around Lee and caressing her breast.

"We'll have plenty of time later. I might even sneak into bed with you tonight."

"That's a date," Lee promised, leaning back against Kay's body. It felt so strong, so right. She hated to move, but family duty called.

They stood on the front porch together as Aunt
Grace drove up to the farmhouse. She got out of the
car and helped Grandma Brant out of the other side.
Lee's grandmother walked directly to the house while
Aunt Grace got a small suitcase out of the back seat.
Lee met Grandma Brant at the bottom of the steps
and gave her a big hug. Kay went over to relieve Aunt
Grace of her burden. Everyone was smiling and saying
hello as they walked up the steps and into the house.

All four women ended up in the kitchen. Lee's aunt
and grandmother sat at the table enjoying some iced
tea while Kay peeled potatoes and Lee sliced up a summer squash and onions. Everyone shared cooking insights while they reestablished their friendship.

Grandma Brant seemed ageless to Lee as she listened to her animated discussion with Kay. Kay and
Grandma were obviously delighted with each other,
sharing old family stories and the latest gossip about
well known friends and neighbors. Lee and Grace were
a little out of sync, but soon joined in the verbal interplay.

Lee relaxed and let supper become a group creation.
Suddenly the big dinner was easy and much more fun.
Grandma Brant supplied tried-and-true cooking tips,
encouraging Kay's experiments with several herbs in
the salad. Aunt Grace took over sautéing the squash
and onions, and shared stories from a French cooking
class she had taken two years before. Lee listened to
everyone, mashed the potatoes, and kept an eye on the
chicken, basting it occasionally.

Supper was delicious, everyone agreed, and the joint
results raised doubts about the old adage that too
many cooks spoiled the sauce. The dinner conversation
was filled with laughing memories of twenty years ago,
when they had all shared many meals at the same
table. For dessert, Lee sliced up Kay's red, ripe watermelon. They all went out on the front porch to enjoy

their melon where the seeds and dripping juice were
not a detriment.

Lee watched Kay talk to Grandma Brant and Aunt
Grace. She admired Kay's ability to reach across the
barriers of age and time to share herself with the other
women. Why does she call herself a hermit, Lee wondered. Kay caught her watching and sent Lee a loving
look that made Lee grin in response. What more could
she want in a lover?

Lee sat back and just let herself watch Kay. Kay's
fluid movements and natural grace reminded her of
the two-year-old filly she had watched in Ralph Hartman's pasture. Kay's movements shared the same
wholeness and balance, a total awareness of her body.
Yet there was the same hidden fire and intense presence that promised an unbridled mind.

Lee felt the physical response in herself as she
watched Kay. Where was all this sexuality in herself
coming from? Kay caught her eye again, and her tender
gaze made Lee want to reach out for a touch. Kay
winked and turned back to Aunt Grace, leaving Lee
wondering at herself.

Why had she suddenly experienced this incredible
desire? She watched Kay, feeling a gentle ache. But was
it just that—an intense physical response? Lee thought
of their lovemaking Saturday night, and her body reacted strongly, making it hard to ignore its demands.
Lee was forced to admit that her sexual attraction to
Kay was overwhelming. Her growing trust and love
with Kay were beginning to break down her barriers of
anxiety and self-protectiveness. Would she be able to
leave her fears behind and act out her desire? When
she made love again to Kay, she wanted it to be like
her dream.

Lee was about to follow her mind farther along this
trail when she heard Aunt Grace announce that she
had to return to Knoxville. They all said goodbye, and
Lee promised to return Grandma Brant to Knoxville on

Friday. As Aunt Grace drove away, Grandma Brant excused herself, leaving Kay and Lee alone for a few moments.

Kay came closer and smiled. "You'd better watch those looks you've been throwing across the room. It might be hard to explain why we need to disappear for an hour or two."

Kay reached out and gently rubbed Lee's back. Lee fought to control her immediate response.

"You're not helping," she answered with a wry look. "Do you have any idea what affect your eyes have on me?"

"Yes."

Lee didn't control the laughter that bubbled up. "I've never felt this way, Kay. Have you put a spell on me or what? All I want to do is get you in bed."

"Good."

Kay's eyes changed and Lee felt like she would melt. Lee looked out into the yard, trying to regain control. As soon as Kay's hand touched her hair, she knew it was useless.

"I thought I'd thrown this all away Sunday, after you left. I felt so alone. Then this morning it was all different again. I feel like I'm breaking through so many walls with you. And, somehow, it's all connected. Needing you so much, touching you, and flying with the hawk. It feels connected, but I can't see how."

Kay nodded her agreement, her eyes still holding Lee's. "I know, Leah. Something very important is happening between us."

Kay bent down with her eyes closed and gently kissed Lee. All of her understanding and her love touched Lee. Lee tried closing her eyes and sending her own message back. For a moment, Lee felt herself spinning in gray nothingness. Only Kay's loving presence was there and her own being. Lee was disconnected from physical reality, completely free of the Earth and her familiar constrictions.

♌ ♌ ♌

"Lee, can you help me a minute?" Grandma Brant called from the house.

Lee opened her eyes, her moment in infinity gone. Kay's dear face was still kissing close. Her deep blue eyes were filled with tenderness and just a touch of awe.

"I felt it too," she whispered.

Lee nodded, caressed Kay's face with her fingertips, and turned to go into the house.

"I'm coming, Grandma."

The rest of the evening was quiet and relaxed. Kay talked about her grandmother and the years they had shared on the mountain while Kay began her study of the healing arts. Grandma Brant wholly approved of Kay's endeavors.

"I'm glad you're back, Kay. Dixie needed to hand that knowledge on. Our mountains are a storehouse of the old ways. I'm so glad you're both back, gathering up your heritage. Your generation is smart to take the time. I could never understand your mothers, but I guess they had other fish to fry."

She turned to Lee to include her with a nod.

"You know, Leah, I've always felt your writing ability comes right down from your grandpa. James had such a way with words. He could make a story seem so real. When I read your article about him in the Sunday paper, I knew James' gift was still alive. I was so proud."

"Thank you, Grandma. I hope I can live up to Grandpa's reputation."

"Don't worry, honey. He's there to help you. All you have to do is ask."

Lee blinked, trying to rearrange her image of her grandmother. Her statement sounded right out of a new-age bestseller. Or was Grandma speaking of angels?

About eleven, Grandma Brant was still going strong, but both Kay and Lee were wilting. Finally Kay stood up and made her excuses. Lee followed her to the front door.

"Do you have to go?"

"I think it's best. You two need to talk together without anybody around. She's wonderful, honey. Maybe we can get together tomorrow. I love you, Leah." Kay leaned forward and kissed Lee. Lee felt the longing and love in her touch.

Lee returned to the living room, her thoughts with Kay. It was only a few minutes before she and Grandma Brant headed to bed.

In the morning, Grandma Brant helped fix breakfast. They talked of her life in the nursing home and her disappointment with the bland food there. She and Lee were finishing up the pot of tea they shared, when she looked at Lee with a smile.

"I was really glad to see Kay Holt here last night. She's growing into Dixie's shoes. I'm glad she's here for you."

"Yes, she's really a wonderful person. I'm lucky to have her for a friend," Lee said, wondering where Grandma was taking this conversation.

"You always were great friends, and it seems to be a lot more now. She loves you a great deal."

Lee looked up in surprise, trying to decide if her grandmother had said what she had heard. She decided it was time to be truthful.

"Yes, Grandma, we both love each other. I'm lucky to have found her again. Some people have problems with that, with women loving each other, but I have to be a lesbian to be myself."

Grandma Brant's expression didn't flicker as she nodded. "I've always felt that to truly love someone and to have that love returned was the greatest gift anyone

could receive. You are both very lucky." Grandma
nodded again and was silent for a moment. Then she
chuckled.

"I remember when your mother talked to me about
you and your women friends, as she called them. She
was so worried about your future and said she hoped
you still would meet that right fellow."

"She did?" Lee was aghast.

Her mother had always seemed cool and restrained
toward her lovers, but Lee had never thought that con-
cealed any criticism of her lesbianism.

"But you know, Leah, Mary was always afraid to be
different or question the rules. That was just her way,
and it was best for her. But I reminded her that we
both always knew you were special, and that meant
you were different. Then I said that maybe part of that
special difference was that you must love women. I
also told her that anyone who loved enough to take the
risks of being so different must really need that love in
her life, and I respected you for it."

"What did she say?"

"Oh, I think she was disappointed in me." Grandma
Brant gave a wholehearted laugh. "I think I was supposed to console her and talk to you, but I couldn't of
course. I tried to keep talking to her about it over the
years, asking about you and how the two of you were
getting along. She said less and less about it, but I
always worried that it might come between the two of
you."

"No, I don't think it did," Lee answered with a frown.
"She never wanted to hear much about my social life
or my friends. She never snubbed anyone I introduced
to her, though. But she was like that with Kenny, too.
Mom always encouraged our school and career choices,
but not any plans to get really involved with anyone, or
settle down. Maybe she felt she couldn't help us with
that after the way things ended up with Dad."

"I always felt your father made poor choices, Leah. You know that. I'm just glad you ended up down here as many times as you did. I've missed you the past few years. Have they been happy ones?"

"I guess so Grandma, mostly, at least at the time they seemed fine. But this last year, since the accident, I've been really questioning my choices. I really miss Mom. You know, talking to her, figuring things out together. We got to be friends those last few years, and I miss that now."

"I do too, honey. She was a good friend to both of us. I'm sorry she's gone, but that's probably for the best too."

"How can it be?" Lee demanded, with a twinge of anger.

"I don't know, Leah. All I know is that years from now you'll still miss her, but you may see that you made important changes because she was gone, and those changes added to your own life. I always wonder if that's how it is for those who pass on, too."

"Grandma, how can you say that? How has anybody's death ever helped you?" Lee let her irritation show in her face.

"Honey, years ago, before your mother and Grace were born, I had a baby that was stillborn. A little boy who looked so perfect I just couldn't believe. . . . Your grandpa took it very hard, he so wanted a son. I think that James valued our two girls so much more because of that loss. I taught myself to paint then, before your mother was born, to give my mind and hands a way to express my emotions. I still paint now. It helps me through the ups and downs, and it's a part of myself I really cherish."

"Well, maybe you're right Grandma. Maybe I will understand better some day." Lee's voice didn't hide her distress. "Right now, understanding is the last thing I feel."

Later that day Lee rode Tellico to the cemetery and
on up the logging road. Kay's Jeep was nowhere in
sight, so Lee assumed she had gone out on calls and
would be gone for some time. She decided to follow
the old dirt road upward until it joined Rafter Road
again. It was over an hour before Lee rode Tellico out
onto the paved road close to McMurphy's farm.

She heard the high-pitched whinny of a foal and
turned Tellico toward McMurphy's. In the small paddock by the road, Molly and her colt were grazing. The
colt walked awkwardly on the tips of his front hooves
but otherwise seemed none the worse for his embat-
tled birth.

Seeing Tellico, the baby started to come closer to
investigate, but Molly headed him off and led him
away. She paused just long enough to snake out her
head in Tellico's direction. The mare's angry expression and flattened ears showed her displeasure so
plainly that Lee understood her message implicitly.
Tellico ignored Molly's insinuation and nickered at the
retreating youngster. Molly glared over her shoulder
and urged the colt farther away. Lee could feel Tellico's
deep sigh as she turned him back down the road toward home.

It took the better part of an hour to wind their way
down Rafter Road to the farm. Lee was surprised to
see Kay's Jeep parked by the house. She hurried
through her post-ride routine to join Kay and Grandma
on the front porch.

Grandma Brant was ensconced on the old rocker.
Kay sat on the front edge of the porch floor, her head
back against a pillar and one leg dangling into the
flower bed. Kay was listening intently as Grandma
talked about her youth on the mountain at the turn of
the century.

Lee went inside to change into shorts and a tank
top, and to wash up. She returned to the porch with
big glasses of iced tea for all three of them. After pass-

ing out the glasses to both women, she sat down close
to Kay. Using the same pillar as Kay to brace against,
and turning her back to the road, Lee sat so she could
look directly at Grandma Brant.

Grandma was sharing her memories of Dixie Holt's
grandmother, Kay's great-great-grandmother. Grandma
Brant explained that Alicia Birdsong had been born just
before the Civil War in 1855, but her early years had
been little influenced by the tragedy of that war. She
had lived deep in the mountains, virtually isolated
from the momentous changes that transformed the
rest of the country by the turn of the century.

Dixie had been born in 1902 and joined the baker's
dozen of grandchildren Alicia gathered around herself.
Although eight years younger, Ellie had often tagged
along with Dixie on the daily excursions Alicia organ-
ized into the woods and meadows. Alicia was the local
herbal healer and used the mountains as her medicine
chest. The children helped search out each leaf, seed,
root, and bark that must be gathered in its season.
Most of the children lost interest as they grew up, but
Dixie continued to climb the mountain each day with
her Grandma Birdsong.

Alicia saw the gift in Dixie and encouraged her interest. She shared all she knew about herbal medicine and
the laying on of hands. Much of her knowledge came
from her mother who had been a healer to the
Cherokees who remained hidden in the mountains.
Alicia also gathered Old World remedies from the
newer settlers in the hills and passed this knowledge
on to Dixie.

Dixie was still a young apprentice to Alicia when she
met Moses Holt in 1918 and fell in love. Moses had returned to the mountain after four months of war in
France, bringing with him a shrapnel-filled leg and mus-
tard gas-scarred lungs. Dixie married him on her six-
teenth birthday, in the fall of 1918. By the fall of 1919,
Dixie had a baby boy, Matthew Holt. She had lost

Moses in the winter flu epidemic that decimated the country.

Dixie turned to Alicia to give her hope for the future and help with Matthew. Alicia gave Dixie a home and a livelihood. Over the following years, Dixie became known throughout the mountains as one of the best practicing herbalists, skilled in healing both animals and people.

In her own time, Dixie took on Matthew's infant daughter from his late marriage. Kay's mother had died in childbirth, and Matthew had left the mountains soon after. Kay grew up on Dixie's farm, absorbing Alicia's bequest from infancy.

"I can remember the day you were born, Kay," Grandma Brant reminisced. "Dixie needed help, so I was at the farm. She took me in to see you when you were sound asleep in that old, carved, wooden cradle. She swore you looked just like Alicia, and she was right. That's why she named you for her, Kawi Alicia Holt.

"Why Kawi, Grandma?" Lee asked.

Grandma Brant chuckled. "Kawi was one of the few Cherokee words Dixie remembered. It came from a phrase Ani-Kawi, the name of the deer totem clan. Of course, Kawi Alicia got shortened to K.A. and then to Kay right away."

Lee sat quietly for a moment, caught up in the picture of Alicia Birdsong leading a group of laughing children through the mountains, collecting all manner of plants and roots. She remembered how Kay had taken her to find chicory and henbane when they bloomed in the summer, and what an adventure it had been.

Kay's voice broke through her thoughts. "I remember Grandma Dixie cursing the fact that she had been taught to read and write. She said that writing things down was an excuse not to use the brain you'd been given. She claimed Grandma Birdsong had a chant or poem or song for just about every concoction or extract she made."

Kay chuckled then continued. "I thought she was just being silly, you know, just complaining about progress. Then, when I was in college, I read a quote from ancient Greece that said basically the same thing. That fellow was complaining about the invention of writing and the loss of oral tradition. By the time I came back to the mountain, I was ready to listen to what Grandma Dixie had to say."

"Yes, I'm afraid we've lost a lot of knowledge to progress." Grandma Brant shook her head.

"Was Dixie upset when Kay left for California?" Lee asked.

"Oh yes," Grandma snorted. "She was furious with Matthew. She kept muttering that he was addle-brained to take a fourteen-year-old girl raised in the mountains and tell her to live in Los Angeles just because his latest girlfriend told him to. She said he must have forgotten how hard it was to be fourteen. She almost fought him on it; she almost kept you here, Kay. But I told her you were too much of a mountain woman to stay away for long, and Dixie agreed. We never dreamed it would be sixteen years before you came home."

"I never did either, Grandma Brant." Kay's voice was low and sad.

The three women sat quietly for several minutes, listening to their memories. The occasional squeak of the old rocker was the only sound on the porch.

Lee turned sideways so she could look out into the yard. The movement of one of the cats that now lived in the barn caught her eye. She was watching the calico cat sneak around the barn door when she heard Tellico whinny from the back of his pasture. Lee could hear him trotting along the pasture fence and pushing through the bushes to see someone on the road. The barn blocked her view of the traveler. Tellico whinnied again just as she made out the clopping sounds of another horse on the dirt road.

In a minute or two a horse appeared, walking sedately along with two young girls on his back. They were talking and giggling as they rode, sharing their delight with each other. Both girls waved hello to the trio on the porch and then urged on their ambling steed.

"That could have been you two twenty-five years ago on Blackjack. You always did have the best time together, laughing and giggling all the time," Grandma Brant chuckled.

"Grandma Dixie said our families have always gotten along. She said once that our families always worked together and shared their gifts with each other. I asked her what she meant. Her answer was that maybe I'd be lucky enough to find out one day. Do you know what she meant?" Kay inquired of Grandma Brant.

"Well now, that's something I've especially wanted to talk to both of you about. Lee, your mother told me to never talk to you about it when you were growing up, so I didn't. But now you're a full grown woman, back on the mountain and with Kay, so I best speak up."

"What are you talking about, Grandma?"

"A gift, child, a precious gift the Brants share with Alicia's descendants. It probably began long before that, but that was what James told me. Seems his oldest sister, Felicity, was great friends with Alicia. She was the oldest, sixteen years older than James, so they weren't close. But he remembered seeing those two together working on a patient. He said it was like watching a dance, an intricate dance, with never a word spoken by anyone."

"I don't understand, Grandma. What do you mean?" asked Lee, her heart suddenly pounding.

"James didn't understand it either, so he eventually asked Felicity about her work with Alicia. She told him she was a translator. Felicity claimed that she could be part of a patient so she knew exactly what was wrong, and then she could give that information mentally to Alicia. She said it didn't work for every patient, but it always worked in serious cases. Felicity also claimed that it was a gift of everyone in the family."

Lee glanced at Kay questioningly, wondering whether to say anything about her own experiences. Kay shrugged.

"Did Grandpa ever have this gift?" Lee asked.

"He said he did, but only a few times. When he was an adolescent, he said it just happened. Suddenly he was a rabbit running from his own dog. That's why he never hunted. There were other incidents that left a deep imprint on his thoughts. The only other time was in the war. All he would ever say about that was what he learned made him a pacifist forever. All his brothers and sisters had moved away before he talked to me about it, so I never got to ask them about it."

"Did he ever work with Dixie, Grandma?" Lee asked.

"He tried, but he was never successful. A couple of times she took him to see her patients, but he never made any connections. Dixie thought the pain and fear of the war had scarred him so the ability couldn't develop."

"That sounds like Grandma," Kay agreed. "She felt fear and lack of trust block the mental or psychic abilities that we all have. She said to heal with my touch I had to reach out with all the love and trust I could muster. It wasn't easy. I had to be depro- grammed from a lot I learned in California. And some- times I am still afraid to reach out or touch."

Listening, Lee knew that the last statement was not just about healing Kay's patients. She reached out and held Kay's hand. Kay turned and gave her that gentle smile. Lee turned back to her grandmother.

"Why didn't Mother want you to talk to me about this?"

"I think she was afraid, Leah, but I'm not sure. She had a terrible crush on your father, Kay, but he never gave her a second look. He was always gadding about, off to Knoxville or someplace. When Jack Kirby started dating Mary, Matthew started to pay her some attention too. Then something happened between them, I'm not sure what. Mary refused to say, but she said she'd never go out with that masher again. So she up and married Jack, and they took off for Ohio. Matthew hung around like a moonstruck calf until they left.

"I always wondered what had happened. James always claimed there was an intensely sexual side to this gift that was a vital link between the two people involved. I knew Felicity and Alicia were close, so I figured something physically overwhelming must have happened between Matthew and Mary. Whatever it was it scared Mary badly, and Matthew took a long time getting over it too."

Lee looked at Kay and rolled her eyes. Kay winked in response and then turned to ask more.

"So Alicia and Felicity were lovers?"

"Oh yes, I'm sure they were. When Dixie and I were children, Felicity was always with Alicia. As we grew older, we understood it was more than friendship. It was just accepted or ignored by everyone who knew them."

"So Mother didn't want me to know anything about this ability or the tie with the Holts?" Lee was puzzled.

"No, she didn't. Mary was sure that if you knew you'd end up in some sort of trouble, or you'd feel some illogical tie to the mountain and to Kay.

"When you two became the best of friends, she was even more worried. Then Matthew sent for Kay, and Mary thought it was settled. I didn't tell her I thought it was about two years too late."

"You knew?" Lee was startled.

"I saw the change in you and how the animals started to reach out to the both of you. And it was obvious you and Kay were no longer children, especially that last year. I kept my mouth shut so Mary wouldn't fly off the handle completely."

"I wish someone had told me about this gift a long time ago. It was scary when I was young, but lately I was sure I was crazy."

"It's come back then, Leah? I wondered when you decided to come back for the summer. I didn't think it was coincidence that you were both on the mountain again."

Kay and Lee looked at each other, astonished at this pronouncement. Grandma Brant looked on with a pleased smile.

"I'd better go inside. I need to look for something." Grandma announced and went into the house.

Lee smiled at Kay after her grandmother had left. "I guess this helps explain what's been happening."

"Yeah," Kay agreed. "Not only are we not the first Holt and Kirby to get involved with each other, we even have lesbian predecessors."

They laughed together, pleased with their new-found history.

"I thought I'd stay for supper, if that's okay," Kay said. "I brought a pie from the Sweet Shoppe for dessert."

"Sure, stay as long as you want."

"I wish I could stay later, but I have to head to Sweet-water by seven to see a friend."

"A friend?" Lee arched her eyebrows.

"Oh now, Sandy and I are ancient history. We just get together once in a while to get caught up."

Lee laughed. "I guess I can I can keep myself busy for one night. I'm heading for Knoxville with Grandma tomorrow. Will you be around tomorrow night?"

"Sure, if you want some company."

"I'd love it."

"Have you decided about the job?"

"Not exactly what I'm going to say to Meeks. I don't think Knoxville is the place for me." Lee was certain, her voice firm.

"What about Maggie? What will you say to her?"

"That's another problem. I know I have to explain what happened and that I'm involved with you. I'd like to have Maggie as a friend, but maybe that's not possible.

"Are we involved, Leah?"

Lee leaned forward and kissed Kay. Kay's arms encircled her. "Silly question."

"Are we going to follow in Alicia and Felicity's footsteps?" asked Kay, still holding Lee close.

"With lots of practice I'm sure we can follow in their illustrious footsteps. But we need to talk seriously about this. Are you sure you want to experience it, to share my thoughts and the thoughts of others? It sounds like it won't be totally controlled by either of us, and it might happen when we least expect it. Then there's this intense sexual link Grandpa talked about."

Kay's countenance remained solemn.

"I think the advantages outweigh the risks. I've given it some thought, and I believe I'll be able to get used to the intrusiveness of the experience. I also asked myself if I trust you enough to relinquish part of my personal control to your judgment. The answer was yes.

"Besides," Kay broke into a smile, "I always wanted to experience the world through the eyes of other beings."

"You've left out the sex," Lee teased, kissing Kay's nose. Kay grinned.

"When do we start?"

"You said you'd be here tomorrow."

"Tomorrow?"

Lee looked at Kay's disappointed face and laughed. "Okay, we can start right now, at least with the animal part."

Lee glanced toward the barn and spotted the calico cat lying in the sun surrounded by her kittens. "How about momma there, or one of the kittens?"

"Ask the mother. The kittens might be frightened by the intrusion."

Lee paused, momentarily feeling guilty. "You know, I never asked for permission before. It just happened. I wonder if it will change anything. Well, here goes."

Lee spoke softly to herself. "I'd like to join the calico cat, if she would allow it."

She found herself lolling on the ground, watching her brood play around her. The scent of the grass rose all around her, a sweet perfume. Lee felt the total awareness of her body, the power and control in even the finest movements. Lee knew the caring love that swelled through her as the mother cat watched each kitten play. One of the kittens, a gray tiger, bounced over and tried to entice mother into play. She boxed him gently, claws sheathed, then held him down for a quick tongue washing. Lee felt the short hair catch on the roughness of her tongue and felt contented as the kitten's coat smoothed beneath her touch. The kitten purred in response and rubbed his head under her chin, then walked away to pounce on his sister. The mother cat continued to watch, enjoying the heat of the late afternoon sun. Lee felt her happiness and her joy to share this small piece of her life with the being that helped feed her family.

Lee was surprised at the awareness, surprised at the open sharing. She continued to see the world from the cat's eyes as she tried to reach out for Kay's mind. Even when the calico glanced their way, helpfully focusing on Kay, she couldn't connect. Lee decided to leave and mentally said goodbye and thank you. The response was immediate and warm. Lee felt gentle, accepting love given without reserve to her as she left.

Back in her own body, Lee sat absolutely still for
several seconds, wondering at the love the cat had
shared. She felt Kay touch her gently.

"Are you back?"

"Yes, yes I am."

"You couldn't reach me?"

"No, just the mother cat. She was so kind." There
was awe in Lee's voice.

"She has no reason not to be. That's their way."

"Cats?"

"No. Everyone, both animal and human, has been
that way to me when I try to help them heal. It's as if
beneath it all there is a gentleness in all beings."

"I didn't know."

Kay merely nodded. "Maybe if you join me first then
reach for her it would work."

"Maybe. I'll try. Are you ready?"

"Sure."

Lee took a deep breath then looked into Kay's beautiful blue eyes. She spoke softly.

"I'd like to join Kay, if I may."

Lee was looking at herself, at her own eyes that
stared back intently. She felt Kay's body around her,
the braids falling down her back, the sun on her legs
as they hung off the porch. She felt all of Kay's body
and the thoughts relating to it, but there was no awareness of her presence, no sharing or joy. She looked
through Kay's eyes and felt her head turn to look at
the cat and kittens. Lee didn't try to reach for the calico's mind. She knew it was useless.

In her own body again, Lee blinked and shook her
head. Kay touched her gently once again, as if to reassure herself of Lee's presence.

"What happened?"

"I don't know. I was there, with you. I could feel all
of you, see what you saw, but I couldn't reach through.
You couldn't feel I was there either, could you?"

"No, but that doesn't make sense. Why would the cat know and not me?" Kay was almost indignant.

"It was like there were walls, Kay. Those barriers, you know? I couldn't reach through. I don't know how."

"Could you with Maggie?"

"No. I just felt her physical self, her sexual need, and thoughts about it that were related to me. She felt a change in herself but never identified that as my presence."

Kay frowned, her face thoughtful. Recognizing her expression, Lee waited for her to explain.

"Maybe that's it, just a question of identifying another entity within your own mind."

"What do you mean?" Lee was confused.

"Perhaps sharing thought is not as unusual as we're taught to believe. Maybe we often share thoughts and ideas on one level and transpose that to our own internal voice."

"What makes you say that?" Lee was intuitively agreeing with Kay's statement but had no knowledge that verified it.

"All of us have instances where we know who's on the phone before we answer it. Sometimes I've talked to a friend and find our minds have been dealing with the same issues, developing complementary answers to the same questions."

"But isn't that just coincidence, or maybe a question of coinciding mental development?" Lee argued.

"Maybe." Kay's face flicked with annoyance. Then she smiled slightly. "The most obvious instance, that I know other couples share, is when I make love. I know when my lover is with me, separate from our bodies. It's like flying. I knew when you were with me Saturday night."

"No you didn't. It wasn't in your thoughts. You never acknowledged me."

"Maybe not at the consciousness level of your connection with me. But I knew, Leah, I knew when we

came back." Kay's eyes met Lee's, challenging her to
deny a basic truth.

Lee dropped her eyes, unable to answer. She knew
what Kay said was almost certainly correct. She also
knew that except for one or two memorable occasions,
Saturday night was her first conscious attempt to sur-
render completely to her lover. How could she deny
Kay's truth when she had experienced what this
woman's love could give? She knew how far she had
traveled with Kay as her guide, both in bed and out.

"Well, I guess we need to think about this," Lee
offered finally.

"Yeah, I guess so."

Lee heard Grandma Brant open the door to the
porch. She and Kay turned to welcome her back.
Grandma Brant carried a book in her hand, one Lee
was unfamiliar with.

"I finally found it," Grandma announced, sounding
quite pleased. "I knew it was here somewhere, but I
had to look everywhere to find where Grace had stored
the books."

"What is it, Grandma?" Lee asked.

"Something for Kay that Dixie gave me years ago. I
put it in this old poetry book. She told me to hang on
to it and give it to Kay when she'd found a Brant to
share it with. Here, Kay, you read it. I always had
trouble with Dixie's writing."

Kay took the brittle piece of paper that was yellowed
with age, and carefully unfolded it.

"A poem?" she asked.

"Dixie called it a song and said it lost something in
the translation. A song that Alicia made her memorize
years ago. Alicia said it would be needed by Dixie's
granddaughter. That she and her loved one would need
it and understand it. Read it out loud, Kay."

Kay hesitated, then started to read in a clear low
voice. "A man will rise up, knowing only destruction
and in his endless hunger poison and strip his Mother

bare. His tears will burn him, his breath will smother him, as Mother's death draws near.

"A woman will rise up, knowing only terror and in her fear and loneliness draw sister near. Their laughter will free them, their touching will heal them, and their loving will teach them that rebirth is near.

"The Children will rise up knowing only happiness and in their strength and loving draw Mother near. Their laughter will awaken Her, their dreams will help heal Her, with kisses they will join Her. Now the Loving Time is here."

All three women sat quietly, stilled by Alicia's words. Kay sighed. "I wish I did understand."

"Me too," echoed Lee.

"I think you will soon. Both of you will soon." Grandma Brant nodded. "Let's get some supper," she added, and they all went inside.

Chapter 13

Lee drove her truck down the interstate, glad the traffic was light. She was also happy to be leaving the city behind. On this visit it had been unbearably hot, dirty, and crowded.

Lee felt the heat sizzle off the asphalt and roll in through the open windows. Without warning, the oppressively humid heat of mid-summer had arrived, Lee realized, almost a month before she would have faced it in Ohio. She hoped she wouldn't regret her ecologically-motivated decision to not buy air conditioning for her truck. Fall began to seem eons away.

She reminded herself that despite the heat the day had been practically perfect. On the drive to Knoxville, Grandma Brant had offered to lease Lee the farm as long as she would let Grandma visit a week or two twice a year. Lee had tried to agree immediately but Grandma had declared she must wait until September to decide.

Her meeting with Greg Meeks had gone surprisingly well, too. Lee had explained that she didn't want to move to Knoxville and that she planned to remain in the mountains. At first Greg had tried to convince her to accept, but when he understood her decision was final he offered to hire her as a stringer for the newspaper. She would cover any assignments in her own area and write a monthly summary. Lee could also submit any local color or historical pieces she had written at a set rate. Although the money was much less than Greg's original offer, Lee accepted it immediately. With the arrangement in combination with her grandmother's offer, Lee suddenly felt a new future opening before her.

Her final visit in Knoxville with Maggie Brown had been the hardest, but ended on a happy note. She had called Maggie earlier and planned to meet for lunch. Maggie had greeted her with a big grin, and they had walked to the same restaurant and found a quiet table.

Their conversation was easy and fun, just as it had been ten days before, at least until Lee brought up their first meeting. After several carefully lighthearted repartees, they came to the mutual conclusion that the previous Tuesday night's encounter was an aberration in an otherwise promising new friendship, and they went on to discuss easier topics.

Maggie talked about her friends in Knoxville, and Lee told her of the surprising number of lesbians near her new home. They finally spoke of their lovers, and Lee waxed poetic as she spoke of Kay. Maggie laughed at her enthusiasm and admitted that her own year-old relationship was disintegrating rapidly. But it was probably for the best, she continued, since they were both moving in opposing career directions.

Maggie had an idea for a series of articles about the Gatlinburg and Pidgeon Forge that she thought would be fun to collaborate on with Lee. Lee agreed enthusiastically and invited Maggie up to the farm for a planning session.

Once more it was after two when Maggie headed back for the newspaper office. Lee had again felt the excitement of talking with her, but this time was it tempered with the knowledge that she no longer wanted to lead the life Maggie still found so compelling.

As she turned off the interstate and drove east on a state road, Lee considered her future. She would continue to write and probably have time to start her novel. At the same time, she had her new relationship with Kay and the abilities they apparently shared. Lee tried to puzzle out why she couldn't reach through to Kay's mind. How had Alicia and Felicity connected mentally with each other? Did Felicity have a secret method or possess a greater gift?

Maybe there was a clue in Alicia's song, Lee reasoned. How did the second verse go? ". . . their touching will heal them and their loving will teach them that rebirth is near." Now what the hell did that mean? She was sure it was important, or Dixie wouldn't have been so specific about Alicia's instructions. Lee continued to ponder the words as she drove.

Lee was driving up Rafter Road much sooner than seemed possible. Looking at her watch she was surprised to find it was just three-thirty. She turned onto the dirt road that led to the farmhouse and was disappointed not to find Kay's Jeep parked in the yard. The absence was not surprising though, Lee admitted, because Kay had had five calls to make this afternoon.

♌ ♌ ♌

After she changed and had a cold drink, Lee walked out back. Trying to find a comfortable spot, she ended up sitting on the roots of the old maple by the spring. She started to think through her aborted attempt to reach Kay's mind. Why would a cat be aware of her mind's presence and not a human?

What are the differences between their two minds, Lee asked herself. Not as much as she used to assume, she admitted. The cat was just as focused, loving, and caring, but she had fewer barriers. The cat's senses included the acknowledgment of the surrounding environment as part of her being. But the human mind seemed to have put up barriers and divided itself from the environment and, to some extent, even from its own body.

There it is again, Lee thought, barriers. Kay's barriers, her own barriers, her own fears seemed to block her use of this gift. What did she really fear? Loss of self. Yes, but not just a loss of identity within another, Lee admitted honestly to herself, remembering her dream. She also feared loss of self-control, especially physically. Admit it, especially sexually.

How could she learn to reach out, to trust, if that fear was always there? How could she break through barriers if she was afraid at all?

Lee paused, trying to come from a new angle. Maybe she could reach out, really share, if she tried it first with a being that didn't arouse those fears. But what living being would not threaten her physical or emotional aspects? Lee leaned back against the maple wondering what to look for. Then she laughed aloud.

A tree! This tree! If she could reach through to this tree, if she could really connect with such a different being, she could learn how to reach Kay.

Lee decided to give it a try. She settled back against the tree trunk with the roots extending out on either side of her. She tried to reach out mentally, feel the rhythms of the tree, and join them. In a few minutes, she was practically asleep.

"This won't work," Lee muttered, and tried another method. "I want to join this tree, share its feelings if it will allow it."

Lee waited with closed eyes, but she didn't try to reach out. She was waiting for the tree to touch her. When it came, it was gentle and caring and held a sweet recognition of Lee as an old friend. She was suddenly behind herself yet still within herself. As the tree she reached out with her life force, and as the human she felt the force embrace her. She envisioned herself surrounded by green, glowing light. It was as if some-

one had reached out and lovingly hugged her. The
feeling was just as warm, just as sensual.

Lee felt the invitation extended and agreed to join
the tree in its life space. Gradually her human identifi-
cation slipped away, and she felt all of her body, all of
her mind and emotions, as the tree. In her trunk was
her strength and the pulsing fibers that kept her body
balanced. Lee could listen and feel the flow of nutrients and water upward as well as food products going
downward.

Lee focused on her roots. She felt her human body
between two of them, and she followed one on down
into the soil. It burrowed deep into the earth, dividing
as it got smaller. All around the dirt was a warm and
living partner with which the root shared space. Between them, the continuous exchange of their most
intimate needs allowed no physical or mental barriers.
They trusted completely to enjoy this joint existence.
There was no question of self-protection or self-
aggrandizement, just total cooperation.

Lee turned upward, following the branches skyward.
She felt the branches sway and felt even the thick
trunk flex minutely in the summer breeze. She understood that the branches were passages for food, water
and nutrients, but they also gave the tree its dancing
response to the wind and weather. Without that sway,
the leaves could not be part of the wind, nor the trunk
remain rooted in the ground.

In the leaves, Lee found joy incarnate. They danced
and swirled with the wind, sharing their breath. The air
offered everything in its power back to them with no
restraint. The rain fell on them and washed them
clean. The sunlight kissed and caressed them throughout the day. Then the moon and the stars enfolded
them at night. Through it all, the leaves danced and
celebrated, creating energy for the entire maple to use.

Finally Lee relaxed and felt all of the tree's physical
and spiritual being. She was overwhelmed by the

intensity of the tree's every moment and the joy it found in sharing with all the world around it. She allowed the sensuality of its entire being to become a part of her. She celebrated its strength, its beauty and uncompromised vitality. Such a range of physical response from the dampened soil to the sunlit breeze seemed impossible in one entity. Only complete and total trust of its own self and the world around it allowed such a being to exist.

Lee felt the tree's life force around her. It reveled in this sharing. It was delighted with her existence and her need to share. Its warmth and unquestioning love pulsed through her being, sharing all its emotions with no reservation. In that moment Lee realized the tree was giving her love just as surely as any human lover ever had. Feeling all this within and around her, Lee's unrestrained answer was to return to the tree all the love and trust in her being. Barriers down, she became one with the tree and lived within it.

The sunlight had begun to change when Lee realized vaguely that it was time to withdraw. She struggled hard to comprehend just how much time had passed, because within the old maple's consciousness it had been a few fleeting moments. She was reluctant to withdraw because of all that needed to be learned. But she understood that time limitations were only of her own making.

The sound of Kay's Jeep made her decide. She slipped into human form as Kay called from the back door.

"Lee, are you out there?"

"Just a moment, I'll be right in."

Lee got up, marveling at how mobile and flexible she felt. She touched the maple's trunk lightly. "Thank you."

ॷ ॷ ॷ

Lee met Kay at the back door.

"It was the strangest thing," Kay said. "I looked past you at least three times, but I couldn't focus on you." Lee just nodded, not wanting to explain as yet. "Let's get some supper," she suggested.

Kay had already eaten, so she talked about her day while Lee made and ate supper. Her calls had been routine checks of both human and animal patients. "I stopped at McMurphy's today, too. Molly's colt is really coming along. His legs still need to stretch out a bit, but I think he'll end up just fine. Doris has worked a lot with him, so he's real confident with people. He had no problems with me giving him the once over."

"I hope Doris realizes how lucky she was to have you there."

"She does. And I know how lucky I was to have you along. Speaking of you, how'd your day go?"

Lee smiled and launched into the tale of her day in Knoxville. Kay was pleased as Lee was with her day.

"I'm glad you invited Maggie up to visit. I'd like to meet her since you like her so much. I just hope she doesn't decide to become a country girl and stay. I don't want any competition just yet."

"Don't worry about that. Maggie loves Knoxville and could never live here. It'll be fun to work with her, though. But what about me leasing the farm? Do you think you can stand to have me for a long-term neighbor?"

"I'd like to have you any way I can."

They laughed together and continued to talk. Kay asked why Lee had been sitting by the spring. Lee's hesitation to answer made Kay look at her in surprise and reevaluate what she had seen.

"Did you try to cross over with someone?" At Lee's nod she asked, "Who? A bird or something?"

"The tree, the maple tree."

"The tree?" Kay paused, her face internally focused. "I never thought about a tree. It must have been very weird; we're so different."

Lee looked out the window and answered very quietly. "It was one of the most astonishingly beautiful experiences I've ever had."

Kay sat still, staring at Lee, trying to assess what she was being told. Her quiet intensity drew Lee back to her. Lee looked into Kay's eyes and tried to answer the question there.

"I joined the maple and was part of it for hours. I can't explain exactly what happened. We were sharing as one being, yet we stayed apart at the core. We celebrated each other, our sharing, our difference, our separation." Lee fell silent still grappling for words to translate her journey.

"Why the tree?"

"I needed to join a being that didn't threaten me or my ideas of physical or emotional control. I chose a tree and ended up understanding what sensuality truly means." Lee paused, and shook her head as she smiled at Kay. "But I understand now. I understand that there can be no barriers between those that share and love. No barriers at all."

Kay looked at Lee, her face a mixture of inquiry and wonder. It was a minute or more before she asked her question.

"No barriers at all, yet you are separate? I don't understand."

"I'll teach you, at the right time."

Lee's quiet expression and the certitude in her voice made Kay remain silent once more. After a few minutes both women stirred, as if reawakening to the present.

"You were right, Kay," Lee stated, forgetting to explain where thought had taken her. Seeing Kay's bewilderment, she smiled and offered more.

"We do all connect subconsciously—for want of a better word. We share ideas and observations constantly with each other, as well as with all the beings around us. I got the distinct impression that the concept of the complete individual independence, as expressed by humanity, is a continuing experiment in denial. We are individuals at our core. But we are also interlocked and enmeshed with all life around us, just as the maple tree is entwined with the soil and air. Anyway, this explains my gift: I merely process the information I receive from people around me differently."

"That sounds like how I heal." Kay nodded thoughtfully.

"I accept the information I'm given by the individual and work from there. It's as if we broadcast what is available for others to know."

"So I only have access to what a being shares with all of life. I don't read minds; I'm not that intrusive. I'm like a radio receiver, but my mind allows the messages to be heard consciously," Lee concluded.

"What about the link between you and me? Grandma Brant's explanation made it sound a bit more complex," Kay questioned.

"It is, I think, but it's based on the same principles. We'll find out when we try it, I guess."

Lee tried to ignore Kay's impatient gaze that wordlessly suggested now was as good a time as any.

"At the right time." Kay's blue eyes danced as she challenged Lee's solemnity.

"Yes, at the right time." Lee chuckled, giving in at last.

"What did you plan for tonight?" Kay asked, still smiling suggestively.

Lee looked up at the kitchen clock that read eight-thirty. She grinned at Kay impishly.

"Let's go up the ridge to the meadow. We can take a blanket and sit and watch the sunset. Unless you think the bugs will be too bad."

"No, it's been a dry spring. It sounds great. I haven't been there since we were fourteen."

"I walked up once. The trail is overgrown, but the meadow is still beautiful. I'll get a blanket."

♌ ♌ ♌

They started up the ridge, following an old path that wasn't more than a faint memory at times. Lee pushed herself to keep up. She was aware that her left leg felt strong and sturdy, unlike the first time this summer when she had climbed the ridge.

When they reached the meadow, the sky was full of orange clouds that faded to mauve away from the setting sun. The deepening blue of the sky behind them made the contrast breathtaking. The sun itself was a bright yellow gold; then it turned almost orange as it set, with the gilded sky all around it.

Lee and Kay stood together, shoulder to shoulder, watching the changing designs. Occasionally one of them would point out a pattern of color that pleased her. After the sun dropped below the western horizon, both women sat on the blanket they had brought up to watch the stars appear. The moon was full and came up early, its silver light hiding all but the brightest stars in a third of the sky.

Lee was lying on her back with Kay's arm under her head watching the colored glimmer of the stars. Blue, red, white, yellow, like distant flowers in a meadow of blackness. She wondered what it felt like to know the stars so well that a person made up stories about them as they wheeled over her. As if sharing her thoughts, Kay broke the silence. "This is the kind of night when it's easy to find the constellations because the dimmer stars don't show up. Look, there's the Big Dipper. I think that's Taurus, and there's Aries. That big red star there, real low in the sky almost on the horizon, is Betelgeuse, part of Orion."

"Orion has always been my favorite," Lee said. "I miss seeing him in the summer sky."

"Yeah," Kay agreed. "It's like a friend is home when Orion's back in the sky. Lately though I've decided it

was probably called Artemis the Huntress before everything got renamed. So I keep trying to say Artemis
more."
    "I'll bet you're right. That feels better to have
Artemis there. It's like having a watchful Amazon in
the sky."
    They lay together quietly a few more minutes.
Suddenly Kay shifted and rubbed her shoulder.
    "What is it?" Lee asked.
    "Somebody just bit me," Kay said ruefully.
    "Maybe we'd better head back."
    "Well, we'd better sit up at least," Kay chuckled.
"They've decided I'm tasty."
    Lee smiled and left a suggestive reply unsaid. She
offered a memory instead. "Do you remember when we
camped out here, that last summer? We stayed up all
night telling stories."
    "Yeah, I remember," Kay's voice was full of laughter.
"We fell asleep just before dawn, and your grandpa
came up about nine in the morning to find out where
we were."
    "I didn't hear the end of it all summer. Grandpa
teased me about keeping bankers' hours until fall when
I went back to Cleveland."
    "I must confess it was quite a thrill to spend the
night together up here," Kay continued. "I thought
about it for months afterward."
    "I always think of that night when I hear Kate
Clinton's routine about going to a slumber party,"
Lee admitted. Kay joined her laughter.
    "I guess we'd better head back down to the house,"
Kay said. "The mosquitoes are really after me now."
    "Yeah, I guess so."
    The women got up, then paused once more to gaze
skyward. At that moment, a meteor blazed across the
night sky. As it tore through the atmosphere, it left a
flash of silver-white light in its wake that took on ruby
red glow at the horizon.

"We saw a shooting star together, Kay. That means you should kiss me."

"What?" Kay was startled.

"Kiss me!"

Kay did as she was told. At first their kiss was gentle and tentative. Then Lee wrapped her arms around Kay and held her tightly. Kay responded. Her kiss deepened, her tongue searched and played with Lee's lips. Kay's hands fell lower and she drew all of Lee's body against her.

Lee felt her body warming with desire. She pulled up Kay's T-shirt and let her hands move across Kay's back. Kay's skin was silken warmth, and Lee felt Kay's muscles moving under her hands. She tightened her hold.

Kay moved slightly so her thigh slipped between Lee's legs. The heat from Kay's body seared through Lee's jeans.

Lee pulled back, trying to think for a moment. In the light of the rising full moon, she could see Kay's face. Desire and need were plain to see, but she saw love and trusting tenderness as well. Lee was undecided whether to reach out and share her new understanding until Kay touched her face with a gentle caress.

"I love you. I can wait until it's right for us both," Kay offered, honoring the indecision she read in Lee's stance.

Lee smiled, knowing her body, Kay's, the night, and all of the meadow and woods as a part of herself. The living joy about and within her spoke of no restraint. She kneeled back down on the blanket, pulling Kay down to her.

"I need you," she said simply.

Kay pulled off her clothes and folded them up along with Lee's to make a pillow. Lee stretched out again on the blanket with the colored stars above her.

"I want to make love with you Kay. I want to share with you, reach out and connect with you. I know I can now, if you want to reach for me."

"Yes, of course I do."

Lee smiled at Kay, knowing she had asked for a gift totally unknown to her. Then she began.

Lee kissed Kay tenderly, allowing all her love to sing through her touch. Her body was across Kay's, and she let her hand wander down Kay's nakedness. She felt Kay shiver with excitement, and she reached out with her being.

Kay was there, searching for her inner touch that would mesh their bodies, minds, and spirits together. Lee encircled her, gathering her in and gently sharing her being with her lover.

As her kisses played across Kay's lips, neck, face and ears, she revealed her mind, her love, her emotions to Kay. Her hands played across all of Kay's body, slowly, tenderly, and Kay not only felt her own body's response but moved with Lee's arms and hands. Lee felt Kay's presence travel throughout her body, gathering understanding, faith and rapture.

Lee moved to intensify the lovemaking. As she did so she sent unrestrained love, trust, and joy to Kay's being, sharing all of herself. Kay's response was instantaneous as she answered with all her love, trust, and being. No barriers remained between them. Merging, they shared their bodies, emotions, and thoughts. They loved and were made love to as one, as their deepest inner beings separately celebrated their joy.

Lee's hands moved across Kay's body, knowing her need intimately. She stroked, bit, sucked, tickled, and caressed, always answering Kay's body. As their passion deepened, Lee closed her eyes, letting her tongue and hands make the choices. She wanted this loving to go on forever. Her body played to Kay's shared rhythms, now fast, now slow, hard and insistent, then gentle.

Kay moaned and took Lee's head in her hands, fingers wrapped in her blond hair, urging Lee's tongue to its goal. Lee's body echoed Kay's moan, as her tongue danced across Kay's clit and her fingers caressed Kay deep inside.

Lee was lost in the ecstasy. She closed her eyes tightly, colors playing before her eyes. Her whole being moved with Kay's to one center point that pulsed with heat. Lee willed the loving to go on and on, so it would never end. She felt herself flying higher and higher with Kay, as Kay's body asked more and more from her lover.

Kay's voice deepened, her moans were low and rhythmic. Lee felt and knew the changes deep within Kay's body. Lee became insistent with her tongue and fingers. Stroking, stroking, her fingers were burning in Kay's heat. Lee felt and heard Kay cry out. Her own body moved with Kay's orgasm, with ripples of pleasure spreading pulsing waves of heat throughout her body.

They held each other tightly, rocking gently until the intensity lessened. Their beings swirled through each other and pulled gently apart. Kay kissed Lee warmly and hugged her tightly. She chuckled a little and then kissed Lee on the cheek.

"Thank you," Kay cleared her throat. "That was astonishing, unbelievable, amazing . . . mmm, you smell good."

Lee chuckled. "That's you that smells so good, silly. Did you enjoy everything?"

"Enjoy? That seems such a mundane thing to say about a miracle."

"No miracle, honey. Just a gift we can share at any time, any place."

Kay was on her side looking down at Lee in the bright moonlight, a slight smile on her lips. Lee looked up at her as the moon's light gave Kay's face a silver cast, and the night was a black cloak around her. God-

dess of the Night, Lee thought, catching Kay's intent
look. She let her being reach out and meet her lover's,
as gentle as the tenderest kiss.

They lay quietly together, and Lee stared at the
panorama above. The moon moved higher. Its silver
light was so bright that shadows played in the
meadow. Lee turned on her side and looked at Kay.

"Thank you," she stated simply, as Kay smiled up at
her. Lee allowed herself to reach to Kay, offering her internal joy and new, quiet assuredness. Kay's self curled
about her, as did Kay's arms, offering warm love and
equal joy. They held each other quietly, not speaking
for several minutes.

Finally Lee stirred. "We'd better go back down, Kawi."

"Okay."

Neither woman moved for a few minutes. Then Kay
sighed. "We'd better go, Leah."

"Yes."

"I wish we could stay here forever."

Lee smiled. "I know, but the mosquitoes are eating
me alive. Come on, my bed is calling us."

They got up and dressed hurriedly. The moon was
still high enough to share its light. The trip down the
ridge was slow on the overgrown path, but the moonlight soon showed the farmhouse ahead.

Lee turned and hugged Kay.

"Come on," she said, taking Kay's hand. "I want to
get you into bed."

Chapter 14

Lee and Kay made love and played together for most of the night. They fell into an exhausted sleep in the predawn darkness, as a few birds began their morning songs.

Lee awoke before Kay. Her sleep had been seemingly dreamless, and her mind felt light and happy. She turned on her side, stretched lazily, and gazed at Kay.

Kay was sleeping deeply, her body sprawled across the bed with the sheet pulled just across her middle. Lee found herself smiling as she watched Kay's face. There was the sweet countenance Lee remembered from her childhood that promised an honest caring and gentleness. There was also the sensuous look of the woman who had shared her passionate love in the moonlight.

Lee leaned over and lightly brushed Kay's forehead with her lips. Kay moved slightly and frowned a little. Lee stayed still until Kay's breathing became regular again, and then she carefully climbed out of bed.

Lee almost laughed aloud as she picked up the shirt she had worn last night. Their clothes had been thrown carelessly on the floor as she and Kay had pulled each other into bed. She put Kay's clothes on the chair and threw hers into the hamper. Then she picked out an-

other pair of shorts and a T-shirt and shut the drawer
quietly.

Lee walked out to the kitchen and started a tea kettle of water. Sunlight streamed through the kitchen windows, and the birds' songs seemed to invite Lee
outside. She wandered out the back door and stopped
to look at the morning.

All around Lee, the bright green abundance of summer danced in the sunny morning light. Above her, the
deep blue sky was dotted with a few puffy, white
clouds. The sunlight had a golden tint that made the
green of the trees more brilliant. Around the honeysuckle bushes the air was so moist it seemed to shim-
mer. Across Tellico's pasture, the morning mist rose
slowly, burning off in the sunlight.

Lee felt like dancing. She tried a few steps but gave
it up with a laugh. The long grass had grabbed her an-
kles, tripping her up. The world was beautiful and
happy, and she was a part of it. Lee whirled around,
hugging herself. She stopped and grinned foolishly at
Kay who was standing on the back steps watching.

"Your water's boiling," Kay called out.

She smiled broadly as Lee walked toward her. Kay
had found a pair of Lee's running shorts that stretched
enough to fit her larger frame. She hadn't bothered
with a shirt, and Lee could see the remnants of last
night's mosquito bites.

"Feeling good today?" Kay asked, continuing to smile.

"I feel wonderful! And you're looking pretty good
yourself," answered Lee, casting an appreciative glance
at Kay's brown breasts. She stepped up to the back
door and gave Kay a quick good morning kiss. She
stepped back again and mirrored Kay's smile.

"We have a problem, lover," Lee cautioned. "There's
absolutely no food for breakfast except Shredded
Wheat."

"I know. That's why I came looking for you. There's
not even enough milk for both of us. But we're in luck.

Doris McMurphy gave me a thank-you loaf of cinnamon bread yesterday. Let's go up to my place and I'll cook."

"That sounds super."

They went inside to gather up Kay's clothes and turn off the kettle. Lee gave Kay an old, stretched-out T-shirt that was just big enough for her. She nodded in approval at the thin material that barely hid Kay's breasts.

"You should dress like that more often."

Kay snorted. "I have enough trouble with George Hankey as it is. He'd want to run off to Knoxville with me if he saw this."

They hopped in Kay's Jeep to drive to the Holt farm. At the barn, Lee had Kay stop. She fed Tellico and checked his water. She promised to see him later and then ran back out to the Jeep.

"Let's go. I'm famished."

Kay nodded and popped the clutch. The Jeep's tires spat back stones as they dug into the gravel road. They sped on up the road and turned onto Rafter. In minutes the Holt farm was in sight.

The bread was heavenly. Lee found herself eating tremendous quantities, along with the eggs and fresh ground coffee Kay prepared.

"I don't know why I'm so hungry," Lee said, half-apologetic.

Kay laughed. "I've always noticed that good sex makes everything taste great. Don't worry, I'm sure we'll burn up lots of calories today."

Lee joined in her laughter, as Kay's look became overtly seductive.

After breakfast, Kay and Lee walked to the barn to feed Kay's mare. Dancy whinnied her impatience. As Kay was feeding, Lee looked speculatively up into the three-quarters-empty hay mow. Kay intercepted her gaze and raised her eyebrows questioningly.

"Did you see somebody up in the mow?"

"No, I was just thinking of an old fantasy of mine. You know, a roll in the hay."

Kay guffawed and hugged her.

"I think people enjoy that more in new-cut grassy hay. Year-old alfalfa is out; you'd be all scratched up. We'll have to postpone it until the first hay cutting. Umm, I can hardly wait."

They continued their chores, checking on Kay's chickens and garden. As they walked, Kay followed up on Lee's confidence by sharing several fantasies of her own. Soon they were laughing together, holding hands, walking back to the house.

A few minutes later back in the kitchen, Kay was wiping the last of breakfast's crumbs off the old, cherry table when Lee came up behind her.

"Stop working immediately," Lee ordered in a stage whisper. She leaned forward to nibble on Kay's neck. She felt Kay begin to shake with silent laughter.

"I have heard from an impeccable source that no lesbian has ever made love on this table. I am here to make sure this deplorable lapse does not continue. Turn around," Lee commanded.

Kay turned, her blue eyes were dancing with laughter, although her face was serious. "Take off those clothes; then jump up there. We have no time to waste."

The rest of the morning was spent in sexual play. Both women were startled by their own needs and delighted that neither wanted to call a halt to their desires.

At first, they made love as other lovers do. They loved each other while remaining in themselves, letting their sexual passion be the bridge between them. Later they reached out to each other, joining together, sharing all of their beings as they made love.

They played other games with their new-found gift. It all started simply, when Lee moved her leg across Kay's body while the sheet remained between them. Their shared sense of touch made the sensation

startling. They felt not only both their own bodies'
touch on the material but also the depth of the sheet.

On further investigation, they found they could feel
an infinite range of touch as they moved their hands
over the sheet. Lee's hand was above, and Kay's hand
moved below. Together they could feel the weave of
the cotton, the flows and fluctuations of thin and
thickness.

Once out of bed, they delighted in sharing all their
senses. Lee was astonished that each sense could differ
so much between two people, yet verbal language trans-
lated their experiences as the same. Looking through
Kay's eyes, sharing her interpretation, the cherry table
took on a slightly deeper red tinge, the cardinal's song
had a haunting overtone, and the cinnamon bread had
a nutty taste.

Kay was fascinated that they each interpreted even
simple sensory input differently. She asked Lee to run
her hand over the cutting board repeatedly. She shared
her own touch on the board with Lee, and they both
marveled at what each of them selected to note and
process.

This touching game moved on to their bodies as
they touched themselves and each other. They shared
their vision as well as their touch. Each woman saw
herself in three dimensions for the first time and could
reach out and touch her own beauty. Retreating into
themselves once more, Lee and Kay made love, each
finally accepting the wonder and awe she saw in her
lover's eyes.

Even their late lunch became an adventure in new
sensations. Lee was astonished at how sweet sugar
tasted to Kay. Kay loved sharing Lee's sense of smell
but teased her about her craving for coffee or black
tea. They finally withdrew to their own bodies so they
could eat in peace.

℥ ℥ ℥

Kay reminded Lee that she had to travel to Madisonville later that afternoon to see her friends and attend
the Health Services meeting.

"Do you want to come along? You could meet Margarette and Toni. They're a lot of fun. You could even
sit in on the meeting, but you'd probably be bored."

"I can see it now," Lee began. "I'd be sitting there
having fantasies about making love on the committee's
big table; then you'd feel it and lose track of the meeting completely."

Kay laughed and nodded.

"It would be a great table to make love on. We could
just sprawl all over it. I guess you're right. Better skip
the meeting."

"I think I'll stay here, honey, and write. I might even
take a nap."

"Do you have to finish an article?" Kay asked.

"No. I want to write down some of my experiences,
particularly last night and maybe about the maple. I
want to try to put it all on paper."

"Good luck. It'd be hard for me to find the words,
but I know you can."

"When will you be back?" Lee asked.

"After ten, probably. We usually run 'til nine." Lee
wrinkled her nose, trying to mask her disappointment
with her clowning, but Kay saw through it easily.

"I know honey, but after tonight we'll have a month
of nights together." She pulled Lee to her, kissing her
lightly and continued in a dramatic voice. "Think of it,
my darling, night after night of endless passion."

Lee was about to make a laughing reply, but once
more became conscious of Kay's closeness. She leaned
forward and kissed Lee deeply. Suddenly, endless passion was no longer a joke.

Kay took Lee's hand, and they ended up on the old
couch in the living room. They started slowly, agreeing
internally to take their time and be gentle. Touch followed touch, and desire grew. They laughed together

as they rolled off onto the braided rug on the floor. Their sexual arousal flared as they made love sharing their feelings together. As they communicated their sensations, each woman's goal was greater intensity rather than orgasm. Time passed and neither was aware it was gone but knew only their all-encompassing internal fire. Then, together, they moved a beat too fast and let the heat engulf them.

Eventually Lee became cognizant of the hour and realized Kay would have to hurry to get to Madisonville on time. Ignoring Kay's protests, Lee pushed her toward the bathroom. It took even greater strength to ignore Kay's invitation to join her in the shower, but Lee knew full well how such a shower would end.

Once scrubbed and dressed, Kay was resigned to her fate. She offered to drop Lee at the farm on her drive down the mountain. As they drove to her home, Lee found herself watching Kay with a loving eye. It seemed incredible that this marvelous, talented woman loved and wanted her. Kay caught Lee's look, smiled into her eyes, and then turned back to her driving. Lee was forced to accept love's reality.

Chapter 15

Lee felt restless after Kay drove away. She was tired but not sleepy. Working was impossible because her mind was filled with images of Kay and their hours together. Lee decided to fill the coming hours with an adventure, rather than moon around until Kay returned.

After packing herself a sandwich, an apple, and some water, she left a note for safety's sake, walked out to the barn, and saddled Tellico. She intended to follow the old logging road up higher on the mountain. Grandma Brant and Kay had mentioned an old abandoned homestead where distant cousins once lived. It would be an easy ride, plenty of time before sunset around nine.

Lee rode up Rafter Road and found the logging road turn-off easily. The road started to slope upward almost immediately, but Tellico strode easily forward with his ears pricked toward the unfolding scenery. They passed a huge old mulberry tree that smelled heavenly as the plump purple berries hung in bountiful profusion on its low-hanging branches. They came to a swift-flowing stream that was a foot deep where it cut across the road. Tellico walked through it unhesitatingly, though Lee knew the spring-fed water was cold.

The road turned and followed the stream bed up the mountainside. Lee loved the sound of the tumbling stream as it skipped down the mountain ridge. It seemed to be singing an old familiar song, but Lee couldn't quite remember the words.

Eventually the road climbed upward, leaving the creek behind. She rode into a tall, dark stand of mature maples that shaded the road. Lee muttered under her breath and slipped on a long-sleeved shirt as the mosquitoes found her. Tellico stepped up his pace.

After two long curves in the road, they broke into a sunny stretch and left most of their winged pursuers behind. Lee breathed a sigh of relief but decided to leave her extra shirt on as the evening breeze blew cooler.

They had climbed three fourths of the way to the top of the mountain along the logging road in just over an hour. This ridge was particularly sheer as it rose higher. The barren rock and steep climb had apparently discouraged any settlement. Lee had only seen two closed-up hunting cabins as she rode, and she was curious about why anyone would choose to settle in such an isolated spot. She knew from Kay's description that the abandoned homestead must be nearby, so she pushed Tellico forward.

They rounded one last turn and came upon a tiny open meadow. Lee was delighted to see an abandoned house surrounded by a few surviving iris beds and a bent and twisted juniper tree. The front of the house was covered with graying clapboards and topped by a roof of wooden shakes. The windows were empty, black holes, offering no glimpses of the interior.

Lee turned Tellico onto the property and rode him past the house to what had been the back yard. She dismounted and tied Tellico to a tree with a lead rope and then got down her supper. As she ate her sandwich and apple, Lee walked around the outside of the old house.

Lee was amazed to see the back end of the house
was a log cabin. Probably the original home, Lee sur-
mised as she looked at the weather-worn logs. They
seemed sturdier than the front structure, although
there were wide cracks between the logs where there
was no mortar.

There was also an old barn at the back of the
meadow, and Lee walked closer to inspect it. Its roof
was falling in, the main doors were gone, and there
were places where the siding was missing as well. In
the evening light, Lee could see the hand-hewn hard-
wood beams that framed the rafters. Between the
bushes and the tall grass that hid the foundation, she
could see walls made of hand-faced stone.

Lee was about to walk back to her horse when she
glimpsed a break in the underbrush behind the barn.
The branches of a gnarled old apple tree rose through
the bushes and saplings further down the slope. She decided to investigate further. As she walked closer, Lee
realized that a well-traveled path continued down the
ridge a ways before it turned out of sight.

Lee couldn't resist the invitation, so she walked as
far as the bend in the path and saw what seemed to be
a small orchard spreading across the ridge. All the
trees were twisted and bent by weather and age. A few
bushes and young saplings had encroached upon the
orchard, but for the most part it remained grass-
covered and open. Across it, the path continued, worn
deep and wide.

Lee walked back to the farm yard wondering why
Kay hadn't spoken of the old orchard or that the path
that would have beckoned to even the most cautious
of explorers. Lee looked at her watch. It was almost
seven. She could follow the path at least half an hour
before turning back and still have an hour to get back
to her farm before dark. Besides, she reasoned, the
path would probably disappear or become impassable
long before her time limit expired. There just weren't

too many places to go besides straight up the steep
ridge to the mountaintop.

She walked over to where Tellico was tied. His eyes
were bright, and he started to paw with impatience as
she tried to decide. His energetic attitude convinced
Lee. She'd explore the path a short ways at least and
have a good story to tell later.

She mounted Tellico easily, smiling at how her body
had strengthened in such a short time. Lee rode Tellico
past the old barn, where he shied at some invisible
danger. Lee urged him on, and he walked along the
path and out into the orchard.

Lee looked at the old trees and decided they were
different types of apples and perhaps a pear or two.
There were sign of deer along the path and throughout
the orchard. They must have a feast here in the fall,
Lee thought with a smile. Along the dirt path, she also
saw a few large dog tracks and one or two footprints
that looked human. Lee was surprised, wondering who
else had wandered here. She rode across the orchard
on the path, perhaps thirty yards in all, and was
pleased to see that it continued.

Tellico walked along the cleared path without much
urging, following it as it began to angle upward. Lee
pressed on as the path went over bare rock and upward into the deep woods. For ten minutes they
walked across the ridge through a dark oak grove.
Then the path turned upward once more. Breaking out
into the late evening sunshine, Lee checked her watch:
seven-twenty, almost time to turn around.

Before her, the path again slanted upward, still
broad, clear, and inviting. Lee asked Tellico to walk on,
and for the first time he seemed unwilling. Looking
ahead she saw no reason to hesitate, so Lee pushed
him forward. They moved steeply upward, then walked
sideways a few paces, then upward once more. Almost
like a staircase with several landings, Lee thought.

She looked ahead through the sparse trees and saw a grassy meadow just above them. The path obviously led there, and Lee decided it would be a good place to turn around. The path was clear, although it crossed a few bare rocks to reach the meadow, and there were large boulders on either side. "One more climb, Tellico. Just be careful on those rocks, okay?" Lee asked him to go forward.

Lee was looking ahead, up the slope, when she felt Tellico's front legs slip. As he struggled to gain his footing on the bare rocks, Lee tightened her leg hold and dropped her rein hand to allow him as much leeway as possible. He slipped once more, and Lee glanced down to see if she could help guide the horse's movements.

As she looked down, Lee saw a motion in the big rocks to the left of the path. She heard the warning rattle and saw a blur of brown and yellow, as Tellico in panic pivoted on his back legs, trying to turn around. He slipped again, pitching Lee forward, then twisted sideways once more and threw himself desperately down the hill. Lee could still hear the dry rattle as she fell into the boulders on the right side of the trail. Her last thought as she struck the ground was intense disbelief.

$$\Omega \quad \Omega \quad \Omega$$

It was dark when she regained consciousness. Her body was wedged around the rocks, her left arm pinned under her, and her legs jammed up against large boulder below her. The rock below was all that held her on the steep hillside, and Lee blessed it silently.

She tried to move her left arm, and almost passed out once more. Her legs were bruised, sore, and stiff, but they could still move. Lee felt a sticky wetness above her left eye. She brought her right arm up with aching slowness to explore her forehead. All she could feel was a mass of wet hair and a deep gash that continued to bleed heavily.

Lee decided to try to move, if only to ascertain how badly she was injured. She placed her right hand firmly on the rock beneath her and pushed against the lower boulder with both legs. Her upper body rose a few inches and remained there just long enough for nausea to overwhelm her. Lee swayed precariously, retching once or twice, then tried to lower herself. She lost her balance and fell against the rock. The pain from her left arm ended her struggle as she lost consciousness again.

The just-past-full moon was high and shining brightly when Lee awoke once more. She was lying on her back across a large boulder, her head in someone's lap, and a hand held a cup to her lips.

"Just drink this down for the pain, love. Then you'll be able to walk soon. Just a few sips more. I know it tastes bitter, but it will soon help." Kay's voice was low and gentle.

Lee felt she was undoubtedly in the best of hands and drank the concoction down. With one hand on the ceramic cup, she felt the deeply engraved patterns on it as she drank.

Kay held Lee quietly as they both waited for the herbal mixture to take effect. Lee was glad to feel Kay's steady support surrounding her.

"I'm so glad you're here. How did you ever find me?" Lee asked.

"Oh, I knew where you were going, remember? Then it was just a simple task to find where you landed. I never thought that old fool of a gelding could unseat you." Kay's voice was warm and almost laughing.

"It was my fault," Lee admitted with a smile. "He had a hard time trying to get up the rocks; then a snake spooked him."

"It's just as well," Kay countered. "The clearing has always been a sacred place. He cannot walk there."

Something about Kay's intonation and rhythm sounded eerie to Lee. For a brief moment, she felt a touch of uneasiness. Then Kay squeezed her hand, and the feeling vanished.

"Can you get up now, honey?"

"I think so. The dizziness is gone."

"Hold on to me so you can get up."

Lee stood up carefully and was surprised to feel little discomfort. She held on to Kay's arm, and they finished the short climb to the clearing above. Kay encouraged her to walk to the center of the grassy meadow where several large, smooth rocks had been piled. Lee followed Kay's example and sat down on one flat stone with her back to another.

Lee sat quietly for several minutes with Kay's arm around her shoulders. Kay seemed deep in thought and didn't speak as Lee gazed around her.

The clearing was small and circular with long grass covering the ground. The bright moon cast deep shadows from the trees and bushes that surrounded the meadow. From her vantage point, there seemed to be no opening in the surrounding undercover, although Lee knew she had followed a wide, clear path to reach the meadow. The forest was quiet, but Lee could feel the pulse of life all about her.

Lee gazed around and wondered why the clearing was so familiar. Kay's voice broke the stillness with a low laugh, a sensuous sound in the night.

"I was thinking that we should have waited to celebrate our love up here, tonight, instead of last. But here you are all broken up, and I'm wool-gathering around in the moonlight. It was beautiful last night, and beautiful that we shared it with the mountain."

"I wasn't sure you had felt that," Lee said haltingly.

"Of course, love. It's not like I'm not part of the mountain, too."

Kay was quiet once more, her head cocked as if
listening intently. Lee turned to look at Kay's profile,
trying to understand why she seemed so different. It
was as if Kay's thoughts and words were off center,
the cadence and meaning uncertain to her ears. But
Kay's face was so dear, so familiar. Lee reached out
and tucked a few stray strands of silvered hair behind
Kay's ear. Kay turned and smiled warmly at her.

"You were right," she began. "Tonight will be very
special. The magic is as clear and strong as the moon.
We might as well stay the night. Are you comfortable?
Do you need more of the mixture?"

Kay offered Lee the ceramic cup, ignoring her questioning frown. Lee was beginning to feel her bruises
once more, so she willingly swallowed more of the bitter concoction. After she had gulped it down, she tried
to question Kay.

"What do you mean I'm right about tonight? How
can we stay here all night?"

"Hush Lissy. Listen." Kay broke in. "I feel there's
magic abroad tonight that will cross the spirals. We've
helped it with our loving. You know that. Now we must
listen, for it will be generations before even the echoes
of the song will be heard here again."

"What did you call me?" Lee asked in a pinched tone.
Her question was drowned by the wind that set the
trees humming.

Then, in the mountain's blackness, out of the moan
of the trees, came a few notes that gathered strength
and resonance. The music was joined by two deep
voices that started with strong major tones and simple
harmony:

> A man will rise up,
> knowing only destruction
> and in his endless hunger
> poison and strip his Mother bare.
> His tears will burn him,
> his breath with smother him,

as Mother's death draws near.

In the second verse the song changed. A minor key was sung by higher-pitched voices with more intricate harmony dancing through the verse. Lee realized she was harmonizing with Kay's lower tones, and they both sang the verse easily:

> A woman will rise up,
> knowing only terror
> and in her fear and loneliness
> draw sister near.
> Their laughter will free them,
> their touching will heal them
> and their loving will teach them
> that rebirth is near.

The third verse came and swelled through the night. Lee joined the song and heard all the mountain voices sing with her and Kay. Each voice seemed independent and struck odd tones and rhythm. As they sang together, Lee learned what music was to be:

> The Children will rise up,
> knowing only happiness
> and in their strength and loving
> will draw Mother near.
> Their laughter will awaken Her,
> their dreams will help heal Her,
> with their kisses they will join Her.
> Now the Loving Time is here.

The soft silence of the mountain night was around them again. The two women sat silent, holding each other's hand. Kay turned to Lee with a smile and nodded sagaciously.

"That's what we came to hear."

Lee straightened up, pulling away slightly. Taking a deep breath to steady herself, she looked at the woman beside her. She knew now why Kay had seemed different.

"You're Alicia, Alicia Birdsong." Lee's voice was certain, unquestioning.

"Of course, love. Did you lose your way in the song? I'm Alicia and you're Lissy." She stopped as her gaze locked with Lee's.

"No . . ." Alicia corrected herself. "You're not Felicity Brant, are you? Who are you? How did you come here? Don't be frightened. The mountain magic is cutting across the spirals of time, and I'm caught in the magic with you."

Lee nodded silently, finding it hard to speak to this all-too-solid apparition that held her. Finally she stuttered out an introduction.

"I'm Lee, Leah Kirby, granddaughter of Ellie Brant. Grandma told Kay and me all about you yesterday."

"Kay?"

"Kawi Alicia Holt, Dixie Holt's granddaughter."

"My little Dixie? " Alicia's voice was soft and filled with gentle awe.

"Yes. Dixie will be your apprentice—or is. Kay is following her as healer on the mountain."

"And you've come into your power together?"

Lee shivered and tried to pull away from Alicia's soft embrace. She suddenly didn't want to be touching her any longer. For a fearful, confusing moment, she was convinced that her surroundings and the woman beside her were a horrid, insane dream. Panic began to clutch her, and a distortion of her eyesight made the clearing begin to fade to a gray void. Then the gentleness of Alicia's touch reached her thoughts again.

"How did you know that, about Kay and me? Do you mean the ability we share? That's the only power we have." Lee was baffled. Then an emotional squall swept across her, leaving bits of fear, anger, and shame in its wake.

"You couldn't be here tonight if your power had not matured," Alicia assured her. "Why do you look so, child? Are you ashamed of your gift?"

"Yes—no. I must be insane! You're just a crazy dream!" Lee whispered in choking panic. Her vision began to blur.

"Then let the dream happen, Leah." Alicia's quiet demeanor denied the power of her command. Her face was once again, sharp and clear in the moon light.

"In my time, such power is seen as madness," Lee struggled to explain, as her heart slowed to a steady rhythm. "I have experienced a great deal of fear and confusion because of it. Now Kay and I are together, and it could be much more."

"The world has changed so much?" For a moment Alicia's tone held great sadness.

"Yes, you wouldn't recognize it."

Alicia laughted lightly and shook her head as if to clear it. "Perhaps, but my mountain remains. That's why we meet here tonight. It also means you and Kawi have celebrated life together and have known one another."

Lee nodded, no longer hobbled by fear or shame.

Alicia's smile deepened. "Last night you shared your love with all about you, just as Lissy and I did. It formed the bridge we hold together now. There is a reason for you to be here. I know it has quieted many of my fears about the future to meet you tonight."

Lee felt totally at a loss. How could anything so irrational as talking to a woman long dead have a reason for being? She shook her head. Alicia's arm still encircled her, and it squeezed tight. Lee was reminded irresistibly of Kay's strong embrace.

"It's all right, dear one. I think I know. You had to hear the song. We had to reconnect the echoes. We both had to see the spiral running through our lives and on to the Children. Otherwise, we might have fallen to our own despair. Otherwise, I might never teach Dixie, and you might never try to learn the extent of your power."

"The song?" Lee asked. "But why? Grandma gave us a copy yesterday, and repeated your message that Kay and I would need it. It's beautiful, but why do we need it?"

"Because you are part of it, Leah. You are the second verse. You and all the people of our kind are here to prepare the way. The Children will follow, and we will all be back before the Loving Time."

Lee nodded, understanding the bare gist of what was being said. Her head began to spin, and the ground beneath her seemed less than solid. Alicia continued to speak, not noticing Lee's discomfort.

"It is good you chose this pathway tonight. It will push us both along our trails of destiny. No doubt Kawi and Lissy will be unable to return to the mountain this night. Lissy will recognize the magic and be in accordance with it. We must send your Kawi words of understanding and comfort."

Alicia looked at Lee closely, expectantly, and then prompted her firmly.

"Tell Kawi you will see her at dawn, Leah."

"At dawn, Kay, dawn." Lee forced the words past the dizzying haze in her mind.

"Good. Now lean close. I'll hold you tonight and keep you warm. That's it. Sip a little more of the mixture and relax."

Lee put the empty cup down beside herself, taking a moment to stare at the deeply etched pattern of an oak tree spreading below a crescent moon and a star. She leaned heavily on Alicia's shoulder. Her eyes would no longer stay open, and sleep enveloped her.

$$\wedge\!\!\!\!\! \quad \wedge\!\!\!\!\! \quad \wedge\!\!\!\!\!$$

Lee awoke in the yellow light of dawn, straining to hear what had startled her. The joyous morning chorus

of the birds almost drowned out Kay's hail from well
down the ridge. Lee realized that it was Kay's call from
within her own mind that had awakened her.

Lee reached out mentally with a calming answer,
loudly vocalizing one as well. Kay's response was instantaneous in her mind, asking her about her injuries
and her position. Lee answered as well as she could
internally, but mental imagery left much to Kay's imagination. Lee knew that Kay was scaling the steep ridge
as quickly as possible.

Lee rose carefully, suddenly aware of aches and
bruises that had kept silent while she slept. Her head
ached dully, and her left arm sent jarring pain shooting into her shoulder.

Awareness of her injuries brought to mind Alicia
Birdsong. Her face, so closely resembling Kay's, was
clear and beautiful in Lee's mind. For a moment, Lee
felt a deep pang of loss. Then she pushed the feeling
and memories of the night aside.

Lee walked stiffly toward the edge of the clearing
where the path from below ended. She met Kay as she
stepped into the grassy meadow. Kay was puffing from
the climb and had several deep scratches on her arms
from the underbrush. Both women ignored their bodies' complaints as they reached out to hold each other.

"God, Leah. I was so afraid," Kay began and Lee
quieted her with a kiss.

"Did Tellico make it home?"

"He's fine," Kay nodded. "But you look a little worse
for the wear. What happened? How the hell did you
end up way up here?"

"I followed the path, of course. We just went explor-
ing." Lee ignored Kay's puzzled frown. "Tellico slipped
on the bare rock and was spooked by a rattler. I ended
up among the boulders."

At Kay's startled and confused look, Lee sighed. It
seemed impossible to explain it all. Her body's injuries

were clamoring for attention, and a deep tiredness
threatened to overwhelm her.

"Maybe we could start for home? I can explain then,
honey. It's a long, strange story, and I need a couple of
aspirin and some sleep."

Kay's face was instantly filled with concern and sympathy. "Sure. I'm sorry, Lee. Let's get you home and
feeling better, before I give you the fifth degree. Let's
go down to the Jeep. I drove it as close as I could before it got so steep. I'll go first, and you can hold on to
me if you want. Be careful. There isn't much of a path."

Lee almost laughed at Kay's overprotectiveness, as
she thought of the broad path Tellico had followed so
easily. But as she started to walk down the hillside, her
laughter changed to confusion. Her wide, clear path
was now the barest rabbit run that showed the destruction of Tellico's speedy departure. How could that be,
Lee wondered, as she picked her way around a wide,
thorny bush.

Finally, after long minutes of slow descent over the
steep overgrown trail, they reached more level ground
where Kay had left the Jeep. Lee's mind was no longer
wondering about last night's adventure. She was just
trying to control the agony swelling up from all of her
body. Kay gently helped her into the Jeep and fastened
her seat belt.

Kay backed the Jeep a short way and then turned
around and headed back to the old abandoned farm.
She drove slowly and carefully, trying to avoid the
worst bumps, but there was no bypassing all the hill-
ocks and hollows. Lee braced her body as best she
could, then ground her teeth through the pain. She was
immensely relieved when they drove out of the old orchard close to the old barn.

Kay stopped the Jeep and turned to see how Lee had
fared. Her eyes scanned Lee's face with a knowledge-
able glance and then offered her a small, unlabeled
bottle filled with a murky fluid.

"How do you feel? Take a drink of this, honey. It will
help the pain. Do you want to take a break?"

"Yes, a couple minutes might help."

Lee drank the herbal tea, recognizing the bitter taste
from the night before. She sat quietly with her eyes
closed, aware that Kay's close scrutiny continued. She
breathed deeply several times, trying to center her
mind away from the pain.

"That's better," Lee whispered, then opened her eyes
and smiled at her lover. Kay smiled back, but her eyes
were still gauging Lee's responses.

"I'll tell the whole story once we're home. It was all
very strange," Lee promised, answering the unasked
questions.

Kay nodded, obviously still more concerned with
Lee's injuries and than the story behind them. She
relaxed slightly, then began to tell Lee more about the
abandoned farm as they sat there.

"Yours wouldn't be the first weird story about this
place. Remember how your Grandma was saying the
cousins that lived here always had strange things
disappearing and bad luck with their crops? Grandma
Dixie told me that Felicity lived here just before she
died and still walks the orchard on the full moon. She
carved the hex sign there on the barn's side."

Lee was confused by Kay's story. She knew she
hadn't seen any carvings on the barn the previous
evening. All she could remember was Tellico shying at
something invisible. But there on the barn was a large
hex sign incorporating a tree, a crescent moon, and a
star.

"Funny, I'd swear that wasn't there last night, but I
know I've seen that design recently. Everything seemed
different last night. Maybe we can figure it out later.
Let's go home."

"Sure."

Kay started up the Jeep and drove out onto the logging road. She still drove carefully, but they made bet-

ter time. Rafter Road felt like a super highway to Lee when Kay turned onto it. Lee could relax somewhat, but still found herself biting her lip from the pain as the road curved and rolled. The farm had never looked so beautiful as when that ride came to an end.

Kay fixed Lee breakfast and gave her a mixture of herbal teas for the pain and to relax her. She refused to let Lee stay up and bundled her off to bed. Kay lay down beside her, cradling Lee on her shoulder and kissed her hair.

Lee felt Kay reaching out to share her thoughts, lulling her being away from the pain. Lee finally gave in and let sleep come.

It was mid-afternoon when Lee awoke. She was stiff and sore, but the long sleep had somehow taken the edge off her pain. Kay welcomed her into the kitchen with a careful hug and kiss. Then she served her a bowl of soup and more tea in a patterned ceramic mug. Lee was surprised how good the soup tasted even in the heat of the afternoon.

"Special healthy recipe," Kay explained with a wink. She paused and asked, "What's wrong Lee?"

Lee was holding the mug of tea before her gazing at it with a deep frown. One finger was tracing the deeply etched pattern of an oak tree, crescent moon, and star.

"Where did this come from?" she asked in a carefully controlled tone.

"I've been meaning to give it to you." Kay began, with a slight smile. "It's a family tradition. Alicia gave it to Grandma Dixie, and she gave it to me. I'm supposed to save it for the person who shares my life."

"Who told you that?" Lee's voice was intense yet soft.

"Grandma Dixie. She gave it to me after storing it for years. She said Felicity gave it to her before her death, with the instructions that each healer on the mountain should keep the cup for her lover. Why are you looking at me like that? It's just an old cup."

"Never mind," Lee answered flatly, placing the mug on the table. "How did your evening go?" Lee asked, rather than begin her own story.

Kay cocked her head and her eyes twinkled at Lee, acknowledging her sidestepping tactics. Then Kay relaxed and began to relate the events of the evening before.

"I felt rather odd all night. I was at the meeting but very distracted. I tried to tell myself that I just wanted to come home to you, but I finally couldn't ignore it anymore. I tried to call about seven-forty-five. There was no answer, so I went back in to the meeting.

"That was when I suddenly felt better, relaxed, and knew you were all right. The meeting ran late, until almost eleven. I started driving home feeling real tired. I was about ten miles out of Madisonville when the Jeep died. It was that stretch in the foothills where there aren't any houses."

Lee nodded, remembering the isolated stretch of road Kay referred to.

"I tried poking around under the hood until my flashlight got dim. Nothing seemed to work. It was about twelve-thirty, and I figured I'd have to sleep in the Jeep until morning. I tried to call to you in my mind, to tell you I was all right."

"Did I answer?"

"Yes, in a way. I heard a very low, firm voice say 'Kawi, Leah is all right. Come for her at dawn.' Well, I thought I was just imagining it, because it sounded a lot like my own voice. Then I felt you. I felt you warm and safe, and sending your love. Then you said 'dawn' very plainly. I relaxed and slept."

"That must have been uncomfortable." Lee commiserated.

"Yeah, but I was pretty tired," Kay continued. "A truck stopped about four-forty-five and gave me a jump to start the Jeep. I still can't figure out what was wrong. Then as I was driving home I got scared to death. I couldn't feel you anywhere. I drove up to your house and saw Tellico grazing in the yard with his tack on, all scratched and dirty. I yelled for you, but there was no answer. So I put Tellico away and came inside. That's when I saw your note and nearly panicked. I knew you were up on the mountain, probably thrown off and hurt, and I'd have to get some help to find you.

"I almost jumped into the Jeep to drive up the logging road. Then I stopped. I walked out back to the spring and sat by the old maple and asked for help. I just sat there quietly for a while. Then I reached out for you, trying to find you. Then I pictured you up by the old farm, so I drove there. It was easy to follow Tellico's trail."

Lee looked up at the story's end to see Kay's expectant eyes upon her. She knew she must talk about her experience, but felt unsure of the validity of her memory. She picked up the old mug and traced the tree pattern once more. Then she spoke hesitantly.

"I don't think I'll ever understand last night, at least not anytime soon. I don't even know if what I remember is real."

Lee paused again and looked up at Kay. Kay nodded, accepting her prologue easily. She waited a moment and then quietly asked Lee to continue. "Can you tell me now?"

"Sure, I'll try." Lee paused, then began her story.

She kept it as simple as possible but tried to give every detail. Feeling nothing but frustration with the limits of the English language, Lee tried to describe her mental picture of Alicia Birdsong. How could she explain this woman who was so similar to Kay, yet entirely different? Her narration stopped.

Lee found herself imagining how she had sat with her back to the stone and looked into Alicia's beautiful face. Lee reached out with her mind to share with Kay the memory of her encounter. She felt Kay's surprised acceptance of the imagery and realized they had never

shared memories before. At the end of her shared images, they both sat quietly. Both women tried to understand the events they were caught up in.

"Maybe she was a hallucination," Lee suggested half-
heartedly, unsure as she looked into Kay's closed face.
She shook her head and continued. "I'm beginning to
think it was all a dream. Nothing is like I remember it
from last night. I felt—no, I knew my left arm was broken. Now it's just bruised and sprained. I might have
just dreamed it all after I got knocked on the head, to
help me cope with everything that's been happening in
the past few days."

Kay looked at Lee thoughtfully, her blue eyes clear
and brilliant. She spoke with care, as she held the cup
she had given Lee and ran her finger over the pattern.

"That is a rational explanation and could be
accepted to answer any questions we have. But I think
rational explanations have been available for everything that's happened to us. I guess I no longer feel
that rational thought offers the only valid answers for
everything in my life. Especially since you've returned
to the mountain. Do you, Leah?"

"I don't know, I just don't know," Lee answered, her
eyes on the old ceramic mug. "I wish I understood
Alicia's song better. She talked about a bridge between
times, and a spiral, but why does that make us a link
to the Children's return?"

"I think I understand that, " Kay hesitantly began.

"Well?" Lee prompted impatiently.

"I believe that to be at peace or be happy in life a
person must love herself, but all of the culture denies
that need. What better way is there to learn to love
yourself than by loving the mirror image of yourself?"

"You mean another woman."

"Yes. But society doesn't allow that either. And, without such love, unconditional self-love, it's impossible
for all of us to be at peace, so society remains frac-

tured, never complete. It can't hold itself together without a center. Instead it has become self-destructive."

"So we become the bridge that teaches society self-love by loving each other and learning to love ourselves. We help heal the rift."

"That's my theory." Kay nodded slightly and smiled. Lee frowned and was about to say more when Tellico whinnied from the top of his pasture. She wondered what had prompted him to call out, so she walked out onto the front porch and Kay accompanied her. Both women looked toward the road as they heard the sound of a trotting horse.

The big, old horse with his load of two laughing girls trotted into sight. They were trying to stay on as his gait bounced them unmercifully. The front rider was yelling whoa, but her laughter left the horse unconvinced. Finally he started to walk, more of his own accord than as any response to his young charges. The girls giggled, waved to Lee and Kay, and then decided to trot once more. Their old gelding sped up and continued down the road, jarring laughter out of them with every step.

Kay echoed their laughter and turned to Lee with a smile. "You know, I'm beginning to glimpse what great changes are coming for us all. Those two girls will see things we can't imagine, even in our dreams."

Lee watched them trot out of sight. Suddenly, like an echo of the night before, Lee heard the voices of the mountain rise in song:

> The Children will rise up,
> knowing only happiness
> and in their strength and loving
> will draw Mother near.
> Their laughter will awaken Her,
> their dreams will help heal Her,
> with kisses they will join Her.
> Now Loving Time is here.

Lee turned to Kay, knowing her lover heard the swelling chorus as well. Alicia's and her own voice were easily heard among the innumerable voices of the mountain's choir. As the song ended, Lee nodded her head, as if in agreement with another's argument. She tried to smile, although tears had gathered in her eyes.

"Maybe rationality isn't always the valid answer. I think she really was Alicia, Kay. I'm going to accept that, at least for now. And I accept that I have a role to play in this world before the Children return."

Kay smiled encouragingly and reached for Lee's hand. With a squeeze she offered a thought, "Maybe if we're lucky and listen well, we will always remember Alicia's song, and the feel of the turning spiral. I'd like to be ready to sing if we're still alive when the Children return. We'll have lots to do to make that day possible."

"Lots to do," Lee echoed as she squeezed Kay's hand in answer. She felt the spiral turn through their clasped hands and move into the future.

"Lots to do," echoed the valley, and a hawk cried as it circled above Rafter Road.

Other Books from Third Side Press

NOVELS

Hawkwings by Karen Lee Osborne. A novel of love, lust, and mystery, intertwining Emily Hawk's network of friends, her developing romance with Catherine, and the search throughout Chicago for the lover of a friend dying of AIDS. $9.95 1-879427-00-1

American Library Association
1992 Gay & Lesbian Book Award Finalist

On Lill Street by Lynn Kanter. Margaret was a young, radical lesbian-feminist in the mid-1970s, her credentials unblemished, her ideals firm, when she moved to a mixed-gender house on Lill Street.

"Watching everyone struggle with her/his feelings, politics, impulses is truly engrossing and a joyful experience." —Bay Windows $10.95 1-879427-07-9

AfterShocks by Jess Wells. Tracy Giovanni had a list for everything, but when the Big One hit San Francisco—8.0 on the Richter scale—her orderly world crumbled.
$9.95 1-879427-08-7

"This book kept me up all night." —Kate Millet
American Library Association
1993 Gay & Lesbian Book Award Nominee

DRAMA

She's Always Liked the Girls Best by Claudia Allen. Four lesbian plays by two-time Jefferson-award-winning playwright. $11.95 1-879427-11-7

American Library Association
1994 Gay & Lesbian Book Award Finalist

Lambda Book Award
1994 Finalist

STORIES

The Country of Herself **Karen Lee Osborne, editor.**
Questions of identity—cultural and personal—abound in
this collection of short fiction by Chicago women writers,
including Carol Anshaw, Sara Paretsky, Maxine Chernoff,
Angela Jackson, and others. $9.95   1-879427-14-1

Two Willows Chairs **by Jess Wells.**
Superbly crafted short stories of lesbian lives and loves.
                                    $8.95   1-879427-05-2

The Dress/The Sharda Stories **by Jess Wells.**
Rippling with lesbian erotic energy, this collection includes
one story Susie Bright calls "beautifully written and utterly
perverse." $8.95   1-879427-04-4

To order any Third Side Press book or to receive
a free catalog, write to Third Side Press, 2250 W.
Farragut, Chicago, IL 60625-1802. When ordering
books, please include $2 shipping for the first book
and .50 for each additional book.

Third Side Press
because every issue has more than two sides.

The book you are holding is the product of work by
an independent women's book publishing company.